Dominant Desires Sexy Stories Collection

VOLUME 38

11 EROTIC SHORT STORIES

TENA SELDAN

Dominant Desires/ Tena Seldan. -- 1st ed.
Xplicit Press, an imprint of TLM Media LLC

ISBN-13: 978-1-62327-569-3
ISBN-10: 1-62327-569-5
eISBN: 978-1-62327-619-5

Printed in the United States of America

CONTENTS

1 CUM UP THE LADDER

It was early Monday morning, and I was not looking forward to starting a new painting job. I am a construction worker. I paint houses for a living, and in the hot months of the summer, it can be a real bitch. I loaded up my truck and headed for the job I had scheduled to start today. It was going to be a bitch indeed. It was a large house with lots of windows to paint around.

I arrived at the house, unloaded my ladder and other painting supplies, and got ready for the task at hand. I usually have a partner, Joey, to help me but the bastard decided to pick this week to go on vacation and chuff off. I got all my stuff together and set my ladder up at the back of the house. I always liked to start at the back. I first needed to scrape the area, and then I'd start my painting.

I got my hand dandy scraper and started doing my thing if that's what you want to call it. Boy it was going to be hot today, I thought to myself as I took my arm and wiped the already forming beads of sweat from my brow. Little did I know just how fucking hot it was going to get. What do I mean by that you ask? Well, let me tell you. This week would turn out to be one of the hottest weeks of my life, and believe me when I say I mean that in more ways than one!

Right Before My Very Eyes

I started to scrape down the back side of the house on the second story listening to the Rolling Stones croon on my portable radio. I was thinking about my divorce and the fact that I desperately needed some pussy. I hadn't been laid in like four months. All of this was running through my mind when I noticed the curtains had been pulled back on the window I was scraping around. I noticed that the owners had left for work. I didn't have any idea anyone was inside this monstrosity. It appeared that this was a window to a bedroom as I peered inside. One glance inside practically made me fall off of my ladder.

I had to do a double take. I could not believe my fucking eyes! There was a young woman probably 20 or so inside the room butt naked. I couldn't believe my luck. She was fucking smoking hot. She had long dark hair that grazed her perfect tits. She had what I would call a perfect body. It was so fucking hot it was almost too hot if you know what I mean.

Her tits were a perfect size not too big and not too small. She had those pink, puffy nipples that every guy gets a boner for. As I looked at her through the window, my cock was growing so stiff she could probably see it through my white painter's pants even without having to look through the window at it. Her legs were lean and slightly tanned, and she had one of those hot tan lines where her bikini went. She was a perfect 10. When she turned around and I got a glimpse of her ass, my dick nearly broke in half.

Her ass was round and perfect for squeezing when riding a cock cowgirl style. I could feel it in my hands now. I could literally feel the warmth and the roundness of it as I caressed it with my large hands. It made me want to grab my meat right then and there and jerk the fuck off. She knew I was looking at her careen around her room looking sexy as fuck, but she kind of acted like she didn't know. That made the whole scenario even hotter than it already was if that was possible. As I watched her, she put on a performance of all performances. She first sat down on a big chair she had not far from the window I was painting by. I had a bird's eye view of this hot goddess. She started to pinch her tits and play with them. That got me another growth going with my already stiffer than hell boner. I swear my typical 6 and a half inches felt like a good 8-inch by this time.

I couldn't help it; I had to rub on the head before it pressed so hard against my zipper and bust a nut right then and there. By this time, the girl through the window was really starting to put on a show. I noticed she was doing something behind the chair as if to taunt me to figure out what it was. I acted as if I was enjoying my scraping and not watching, but I was watching her every hot move. I did have to look away for a bit and do some things, but lo and behold, when I looked back inside the window she was getting it on with a cucumber. I don't mean just any old cucumber either. I am talking one of those big Italian style cucumbers.

I was glued to the window not wanting to miss one smutty detail. This nasty girl squatted down in the chair with her legs kind of like a frog's and slowly but surely slid her half-hairy pussy down on top of it. She had a puss that wasn't bald, but it wasn't a bush either. It was just right in my opinion, and my cock's opinion, I might add. She wiggled down on that cucumber about 5 or 6 times and finally she got that whole damn thing deep inside her snatch. Just then, she looked up at me and shot me a sexy grin that made my cock head jump. By this time, I had my dick hanging out of my zipper sticking straight out as hard as that cucumber she was banging. She stood right up in the chair about then and she seductively licked all of her wet pussy juice off of that nasty cucumber. At the same time, I was slowly stroking my cock head but not too fast. I wanted to milk this hot show for all it was worth. The aching boner felt hot as fuck anyway.

It was time for me to move my ladder and I was pissed off. I didn't want to leave this naughty goddess all alone to play with herself, but I had to keep on with my scraping. I figured if all else failed, I could beat off in my van later. So I got my stuff and moved my ladder down to the next window upstairs. This was more than likely her parent's room or a guest room. As I climbed my way up with now a half-hard hurting cock, I could see the windows were drawn. As I reached the top, there was my naughty goddess fingering herself off in the floor right in front of the window. It seemed my 6 1/2 was going to reach 8 again if she kept playing her pussy with her wet fingers that way. She held her left breast up to her mouth, smeared some of her pussy cream on it, and ate it off with her mouth and tongue. Fuck! That about made me nut again.

She then got on all fours and turned her perfect ass to the window and kind of lifted one hip and looked under her leg at me. She fingered her pussy then her asshole back and forth. Then, she placed her middle finger in her ass and her index finger in her snatch and jacked on both pretty damn vigorously. Her body started bucking like a horse. I could nearly smell the pussy aroma coming up from her crotch. If I tried hard enough, I swear I caught a whiff of that nasty snatch. Then, she suddenly removed her two fingers and licked her dual juices off of them. I was stroking my cock at that time with it plopped out of my zipper hole standing proud. My ridge stood up big and pink and was so sensitive that every time I grazed it, I about shot the fuck off. She walked across the room and I wondered what she was going to fuck on next. She had a Barbie doll in her hand and I could only imagine what she was going to do with it. First of all, she took her tongue, flicked on Barbie's play pussy, and smiled. Then, she put both of the plastic legs in her mouth and got them wet. Then, suddenly she squatted down on top of those Barbie legs and went to town fucking them. She then stood up and walked towards the window with just the blonde Barbie head protruding from her big pussy. She seemed proud that she could hold the doll inside her snatch while she walked. She turned around, bent over, and let me get a huge eyeful of that doll hanging out of her pussy.

It looked so damn hot I started wanking pretty furiously then. My cock was on fire and red-hot. I pulled the skin over the head as slow as I could without busting my load. I could see her swollen and meaty lips gripping the fuck out of the doll's neck. I literally drooled on my chin; this chick was so smoking hot. Suddenly again, she pulled the wet doll out of her snatch and simply started to finger her slippery pussy with one, then two, then three fingers. She plunged them deep inside quivering at every pull out and then plunge back inside. It turned me on big time to see her lush fingers disappear and then reappear.

Suddenly again, my hot little window goddess decided to do something else.

But before she did it, she disappeared into another room. Damn! What a fucking tease, I thought. I quickly finished scraping that window and got to the bigger window on the side. Much to my surprise (not really), there is my nasty nympho getting it on with a shop-vac. Yes boys, I said a shop-vac! She had one of the smaller attachments with a slit on it flush up to her clit giving that red swollen appendage the once over. Her gullet was feeling hotter than fuck about now, I could tell. She was working her puss over good and I could hear some of her hot moans seeping through the pane. I was whacking pretty damn hard on my peter about then too. I didn't know too many chicks that could handle a shop-vac on their cunts, but this tiger could. Her kitty was getting into it too.

I couldn't help it; by this time, I was jerking my meat so hard I thought it might turn bright fucking red and fall off. Then, the naughty nympho walked straight up to the window and let me see as up close as it gets her nasty snatch. The fucking puss was drenched; it was dribbling down her legs and now she had a rabbit toy flicking and fucking her cookie clean off! I could hear the sloshing noise of that wet fucking cunt as she yanked that toy in and out full fucking force. This was one nasty babe.

She said the words "Jerk that muscle nasty man and make it shoot for me and I'll cream and squirt this cunt of mine." The hair on her pussy was drenched in puss cream. She got a sexy look on her face that almost made me nuts. My balls drew up so tight I almost screamed. I felt so fucking hot and I was beating the fuck outta my dick.

She was pinching nipples, licking cream from her nipples, digging fingers in her pussy, eating cum, and beating that cunt off as well. She was such a nasty girl she was eating her pussy cum off of anything she could find. She even licked some off of the floor and made a moaning sound and that made me have my first big squirt. Then, she ate her cum off of her fingers one by one just as slow as she could to turn me the fuck on. She managed to do precisely what she set out to do.

She squatted over a towel and showed me how her long lipped pussy could gush. It was hotter than hot to me. Once she did that, I just had to release a wad of spunk from my prick. It was hurting by now; I was so damn horny. If I kept holding my cum, my meat would probably burst in a very dangerous manner. So I jerked my cock head fast and blasted my first real load all over the fucking windowpane. Her eyes got as big as saucers when she looked at my thick white jizz dribbling down the fucking window.

It was rather nasty, I must admit. She looked at me like it was now her turn to deliver a load. She played her cat playfully with her toy rabbit and tickled the end of her now hot pink clit until I saw white cream covering the hood and head of the clit. Damn, it was too hot to trot. She came up as close as she could to the window and gushed a wad right out of her juicy love box. It splattered on the window in white goo that made my throbbing prick pop off another time. I felt like I could shoot three or four wads very easily if I wanted to and I wanted to.

The hot goddess then began to voraciously finger her fuzzy snatch so fast that her fingers were a blur; in fact, she got her whole hand in there, fucking her pussy to orgasmic delights like nothing I had ever witnessed. This was the hottest display of erotic cream and sexual pleasure that I had ever seen. It made my dick hard enough to crack a block of ice. Fuck, she was one hot mama! She then turned her back to the window and bent over it in an all too famous porno pose and let me see her wet patch from the other angle and she blew yet one more wad all over that sexy window. I busted one more nut myself for old time's sake and by this time the goddess of raunchy love and I had that window soaked on both sides.

I had experienced many steamy pleasures and hot sex scenarios in my 30 years, but nothing came close to comparing to this little rendezvous on a hot July morning. I would never forget this luscious goddess within the window. She was what dreams and lust are made of if you dig me. She was what put the SEX in sex. I needed to have a break after that massive nut fest so I climbed down from my ladder and headed for Mickey D's for a quarter-pounder value meal. I was bushed. I intended no pun. As I drove out of the driveway, I looked in my rear view mirror and I about busted another nut then and there. There was my little sex kitten atop my ladder licking my jizz off the window. I rubbed my eyes and did a double take and looked again. Yes, I saw right. That nasty little senorita was lapping my cum up like a kitten. Fuck, she was hot as hell!

2 VEGGIES IN, DRESSING OUT

I'm a very kinky woman. I will be the first to admit it. I have never gotten into the typical things when it comes to sex. If it's not kinky or unusual, I simply don't want to take part in it. I have always deviated from the norm, and I am not ashamed to admit it. One thing I particularly love that is extremely kinky, is fucking sex toys. Yes! I said sex toys such as large dildos. Every week I get excited with each trip I take to the neighborhood sex shop. I know that I will be picking out some of the most delicious looking sex toys not just for display, but I am picking out some of my best new friends to fuck as well.

I remember it well the day when it all started, my fascination with sex toys. I was 19 and had just gotten accustomed to being fucked regularly, but my boyfriend suddenly broke up with me. I was horny as fuck one day and needed to put something in my wet snatch. I decided to look around the house and see if I could find something to satisfy my hungry cookie.

I looked all over the house hoping to find a toy of my mom's and stick it in my snatch, but no such luck. I guess she didn't like sharing. Then suddenly I thought about where she could hide it, somewhere she never thought I'd find them. I found a cabinet full of dildos and vibrators of al shapes and sizes. Thinking about them got me wetter than a rainstorm. So I went to the cabinet and got the largest stiffest looking dildo I could find.

I carried it upstairs and decided I was about to give myself a good fucking. I lay down on my bed and started working my wet peach with this dildo. Fuck it felt hot as I fucked myself hard and slow in and out making my pussy drip with horniness. It felt so good I damn near creamed in five minutes, but I teased my nasty clit and puss and waited. I smeared some of my snatch juice on my nips and licked it off and the taste of my own cookie almost made me squirt. I loved eating my own pussy cream. I have actually had an orgasm just eating my pussy cum before. Just considering that sweet musky taste of my kitty got me wetter than fuck all over again.

I was so damn turned on that I held that dildo straight up and then slowly wriggled down on it until I buried the fucker deep inside my big nasty snatch. I was only 19, but I had a big 'ol nasty pussy that had been used a lot. I watched myself as I masturbated and fucked that large dildo. I loved seeing my orgasmic facial expressions on film; it turned me the fuck on. A lot of times I would use my webcam and film myself squirting off, so I could watch it later. When I watched it later, I'd always gush again.

My mind came back to the present time, and all of the deliciously inviting sexy toys I was looking at. I got a bunch of new toys as hard as possible. I also picked me out two of the fattest dildos. They feel great with their bumps and ridges especially when you mount and ride them.

I hurried home to try out my mix of sex toy delights. I decided to do some vibrator playing on my moist patch. I first took my middle finger and did some basic masturbation moves. I tickled, flicked, and swirled the head of my throbbing clit. I adored teasing my pussy until it almost burst and then backing off of it. It got harder each time I did it. The clit hood and head would stand straight up like a cock with a boner. I slowly and steadily worked the vibrator in and out of my bald snatch. I watched in a full-length mirror as I masturbated with this hard as a rock vibrator. Just when I thought I couldn't handle anymore, I moved to some of my horny dildos. I stayed in front of that mirror and found a fat dildo with a "handle" on it. It had bumps and ridges all along that part, so I knew my pussy would throb and quake when she felt this nasty vibrator screwing her. I kind of secured the gourd real well so I could slide my drenched cunt down onto it.

This particular vibrator I was fucking was just about to get me off. I was wiggling and starting to bounce and grind. I knew it was time to take the fucking thing out of me before I squirted all over my floor. I have done that before, right before my husband's friend were to be at my house. I purposely left the door unlocked as well, as secretly I would love to have them catch me and possibly get turned the fuck on themselves. I love thinking of my husband having a big boner in his pants for me. As a matter of fact, he has before as I recall.

I was preparing for a garage sale one Saturday, and my husband was off playing golf and my husband's mother was out doing one of her all day shopping sprees. My husband's friend stayed home with me to help me out. I really didn't expect him though. I was busy sorting things and labeling things, and I suddenly became my usually horny as hell self. All that I had to do was see something that got me hot or be reminded of some sexual escapade and I was wet instantly.

Today, I got a glimpse of my new sex toys and it turned me on. Yes it is weird, but it did. I have had my way with vibrators, and they are hot fucks to have. The rough places on them scratch your g-spot as they boink you or as you fuck them. I started thinking about how I needed some meat inside me, and before I knew it, I was wet as fuck and squirming rubbing my lips without having to stick my actual hand down my pants and jerk off. I guess momentarily, I forgot about my husband's friend and when I looked up the man was seething. I could tell he wanted to fuck my brains out right there.

I looked at him, and he looked back at me with an incredible amount of seduction lying right behind his eyes. He had never come on to me before. I wasn't sure what I had done different today that caused him to have the boner I could see in his trousers. I'll admit at that time it got me very amorous and as wet as my snatch could possibly get. I remember I would move and I'd hear a soap dispenser bottle sound and my pussy would pop cum bubbles. I decided to retreat into my bedroom and leave the door cracked to be ultra kinky. If this horny fucker wanted to get off, he could watch me masturbate all afternoon. I took my vibrator and dildo, and I even threw in my best massager for fun.

I get inside my bedroom and started my cunt games. First of all, I took the large vibrator and sucked on it a bit while I screwed the big dildo. I slipped slowly over the top of that dildo until it disappeared inside my wet snatch. I fucked it hard and deep, and I looked up and saw my husband's friend with just his cock poked through my door wanking it off fast. I could not believe my eyes. This man had the biggest fucking dick I had ever seen and I wanted it inside me right then. The way he stroked it backhanded was almost more than I could take. In fact, I squirted one good gush, and he started jerking faster. I couldn't stand the teasing anymore. My pussy was bulging to mass proportions and about to pop.

I asked him to come in and fuck my brains out. He asked if I wanted to get screwed to the wall and I said fuck yes! So he entered in the bedroom and took me full throttle. He banged the ever living fuck outta my pussy as fast and deep as his big dick would go. Little did I know how hot my husband's hot friend was. He was one of, if not the best, fucks I had ever had. He asked if he could eat my cunt out and of course, I obliged.

He put his face between my quaking thighs and man I tell you what! He ate my pussy so good I nearly cried and wailed like a baby. It was an amazingly hot turn on to know that he had buried his face in my best friend's pussy many times since they used to date. I slapped my feet up by his ears, and I humped the hell out of his face and rubbed my cunt all over his fucking beard. The man got me nearly to the pop off stage and he stopped! What the fuck? I asked. He told me to fuck that dildo for him, and he would jerk off all over my bed, me, and the floor.

I was so ultra horny I did as he wished. I fucked my cunt way hard, and before I knew it, I was spraying and grinding all over my bed. He watched on in pure unadulterated pleasure. I could tell he wanted to fuck my brains out. So I let the fucker bang me. He got on top, I threw my long legs up by his ears, we fucked hard, and we fucked like I have never been fucked before. We did it until we were both cumming at the same time. He ground his cock harder into me as he blew his load deep in me.

I finally drifted back into reality and what I was doing right now at this particular moment, and it was very sexy I must say. I remembered as I was enjoying fucking all of these different sex toys that I was having a little "get together" later. I better get to work chopping, slicing, and dicing. Before I did, I found a particularly large carrot in the new one I had purchased earlier. After washing it off, I decided to suck it a bit and think about how I went down on a big huge dick. I would first lick the head and rim and get it all wet and gooey. Then I'd slowly but surely make my way down the shaft. Just the thought of sucking a cock off made me plunge find my big dildo right into my snatch. Damn! It felt so good that in a couple of strokes I was cumming all over the dildo cock.

I removed the dildo from my pussy, and I decided I wouldn't rinse it off again. I wanted my pussy juice to be all over it when I decided to suck on it again. As I chopped up the carrots, I made sure to plunge the dildo one deep inside my snatch, it was like clockwork. I next moved to the vibrator and fucked myself a few strokes before slicing up the cucumbers. This salad was going to be tasty indeed! I couldn't wait to serve it in a big bowl to my friends. The thought of them biting into a tasty bite of my "secret" salad made me wet all over again. I am so fucking naughty it ought to be a crime! After I screwed myself a few times with each vibrator and dildo, I had a big salad on my hands. I then took a little bit of my pussy cum off of my fingers and added just a touch to my homemade salad dressing. After mixing it up completely, I tasted the tantalizing concoction. It was absolutely delicious. I couldn't wait to serve my pussy juices in a bowl for all of my friends to eat. It would be like getting a personal oral sex job from each of them. The sheer thought of it turned me on immensely. About that time, I looked over and saw one lonely new sex toy, and then I looked up at the clock. I had 20 minutes until my guests arrived. Did I have time to fuck that before they got there?

3 CUM TO LIFE

I was almost dreading another long evening of writing. Of course, I loved writing. I am a writer for God's sake, but I had been writing erotic stories for publication for damn near two years solid. Let's just say I am a bit burnt out. Actually, that's putting it lightly. I had a day job too, but not every day mind you. But every night, I worked on my erotic stories for a certain publication that I wrote for, and it was about time I got started tonight.

There was a new issue I was facing every time I wrote these days; I had memory problems. I wake up in the mornings dazed and confused. I would also wake up feeling like I had been fucked long and hard. It had me confused big time. There were other times my pussy would actually be sore from being screwed. It felt like I had been gang banged all night long. I sometimes had wads of cum seeping from my snatch and down my legs as well. But I had no idea where all this cum came from! What's a woman supposed to think when she feels like she's had her brains fucked out but she doesn't know from whom or when it even happened? I would start to remember more and more as the course of the next day went on. It seems as though I would start the story for the next night the one before it would come to the forefront of my mind.

I got my laptop and started to pen my chapter for the evening. This particular novella was one smutty write for sure. I had written all kinds of naughty and seductive sex scenes into it. If you can imagine it, I have written it. I had everything in this story to turn somebody on big time. I had hard ass fucking, pussy eating, dick sucking, and gang banging and much more. If you could conjure it, you'd find it in my nasty story.

I started writing at a place that was particularly smoking hot and orgasm inducing. In fact, every time that I write my dirty erotic stories, my fingers have a way of making their way into my pants and making their way to my horny, greedy clit. Just writing this story made my snatch dick hungry and orgasm needy. As I started to pen about my main character flicking her clit off, I once again got so fucking wet I could hardly stand it. These stories were turning me into a nymphomaniac of mass proportions indeed. Fuck! I needed some big fat cock, and I needed it now.

As I was writing, I felt myself drift off into a dreamland. This wasn't any old dreamland either. This dreamland was filled with hot men hung with big huge dicks and hotter women with wet clits and cunts. I was transformed and suddenly surrounded by 3 other people, two hot guys and one nasty woman. I could tell they had one thing only on their minds and that was fucking my brains out! I was not opposed, I must say. I was so damn horny I could screw these 3 all night long and then some.

Just as that thought crossed my mind, they sauntered over to where I was sitting and writing. One of the male characters started groping my breasts and ripping my silk blouse off hungrily and ravenously. He grabbed my left tit and sucked hard and deep. It hurt in one way, but in another, it felt fucking hot. It made my cunt get creamy and wet, I know that much. The female character walked over to my other side and started suckling my other nipple and turning me on all the more. In my story, I was writing about a kick ass threesome these characters were engaged in. It seems to me that they are ready to turn it into a foursome. They would hear no complaints from me that's for sure.

Before I had time to think, all three of these horny characters were ravaging my sore body, but I still wanted to be fucked to the wall. The four of us started groping and kissing uncontrollably. All three put their ravaging hands all over my body sending me into the grip of sheer ecstasy. One of the guys lay down on his side in front of my face and the other behind me. They both stuck their hungry and horny cocks inside of me at the same time and fucked my brains out.

It felt so damn good being screwed by two hot men like this. It was absolute heaven having 2 swollen, bulging dicks moving in and out of your body like this. The feeling is absolutely indescribable. When you get stuffed in both holes with a bulging dick, it gives a sensation like no other. It is a naughty filling sensation like no other. Suddenly, the dick that was fucking me in my pussy went away and started to fuck the other woman. She was on her hands and knees doggie style getting screwed hard, and while that happened, she went down on my wet snatch.

I must say, I have never had my pussy eaten out as well as this woman was doing it now. She got right down there and wallowed like there was no tomorrow. Her head moved back and forth and her tongue flicked over my slick clit causing it to throb and get a hard on like a horny cock would. Fuck! It felt so damn good. She knew her way around a hot pussy. That is for sure. She flicked on the end of my clit until I almost had an orgasm and then she stopped.

Then the nasty cunt came and sat on top of my face and fed me her greedy snatch. She tasted musky yet wonderful. She ground her hard clit and wet cunt all over my face. She smeared her pussy all over my face. She did it so hard that I almost quit breathing at times. I'll admit I had never been with another woman, but the experience was hot as fuck! I could easily do it time and time again; it was that enjoyable. As she ate my snatch, one of the men banged her hard from behind giving her everything he had and then some.

This foursome was turning out to be one of the wildest sexcapades I had ever experienced in my life! Just about the time that I decided I was starved for the taste of a hot cock, one of the men gently nudged the woman off of my face and plunged his hard as steel dick in my mouth. The other guy plunged his rod in the woman's mouth. This was becoming almost too hot and spicy for words. It was that naughty and that kinky. I could taste the woman's pussy all over the cock I was slurping as it slipped and slid in and out of my horny mouth. Her pussy tasted tantalizing and downright hot all over his member. I could not get enough of it. I engorged myself on it. I craved it. I drank of the divine pre-cum like I was a thirsty villager in the middle of a hot desert with no water.

Just as the cock I was licking and sucking was about to squirt off, he removed his dick and the two men switched places. Suddenly, I found the other cock thrust deep down my throat gagging me for all it was worth. I could not believe the magnitude for which this cock was thrusting and pounding my mouth. It was all that I could do to take yet another breath. But it was deeply erotic nonetheless.

Suddenly, I feel myself starting to wake up, and I could see the faintest hint of sunlight coming through my curtains. I was very groggy feeling, and my body was sore as hell! I could vaguely remember a few bits and pieces of last night, but only slightly. It was all a hazy memory to be honest. I know one thing for certain. I reeked of sex! I could smell pussy and dick all over me.

I smelled like I walked right out of a brothel or something. I literally had sticky dick cum all stuck in my hair on my head and on my snatch. My face also felt sticky and smelled of sex. I could tell I had been involved in some kind of hot rendezvous, that's for sure. I could tell (and somewhat remember) that I had done it with more than one person. Also, by the smell of my fingers, I could tell that one of those people was a woman.

As I finally started to wake up completely, I looked at my laptop and saw my manuscript was open from the night before. The words I had penned rang a huge bell actually more like a gong in my brain as they always did as of late. I had written about 3 very hot characters, two men and one woman. In the story, they had also taken part in a four-person orgy with another woman. That seemed very familiar to me I must admit. As I was standing there reading my story I had written, I felt something trickling down my leg.

It was cum. It was obvious, it was. At that moment, I knew there was something wrong. I knew I was involved in some sort of mystical or mysterious situation that I had no control over. I also knew that it took place at night when I started to write my erotic stories. I got ready and went to my day job anticipating what the evening would bring.

I got home in the evening sore as hell from seemingly the night before. I ate my dinner and got my head in order for what I was going to write next in my novella. It was going to be steamy that's for sure, and part of me wondered if I wasn't subconsciously making it that way for my own sexual gain. I smiled coyly as that thought entered my mind and I sat down with my laptop to write.

As I started to type, the thoughts of sex and lust came flooding my mind. I could hardly write fast enough, and suddenly, I started to drift away in another hazy state of lust-filled dreams. As I started to write, the four lovers were at in full throttle. Both women, me being one of them of course, side by side on hands and knees getting it in the ass from behind. I had never been a huge anal sex fan, but this felt amazingly good yet rough.

I didn't know I enjoyed anal intercourse so much until now. The way the man pounded my ass from behind felt intoxicating. He thrust his cock in my ass hard and strong. I loved it, I must admit.

It felt amazing and very good. He took his cock out of my ass, threw me down on my back, and plunged it down my hungry throat. He practically stopped my breathing with the blunt force of his dick. He plunged in and out and in and out until he came down my throat in huge spurts. I then thought maybe he was done with me, but he begged me to fuck him hard reverse cowgirl style. As I banged him hard cowgirl style, he yanked my ponytail hard and begged me to screw him faster and harder. He even said "Giddy up cowgirl" as I banged his steel rod as hard as I could possibly fuck it.

The woman stood up in front of my face and thrust her hairy snatch in my mouth as I reverse cowgirl fucked the guy. Her pussy tasted like a concoction of dick, sex, pussy, and musk. I will admit it turned me on and brought me to an orgasm that flooded the guy's lap and cock. Just as I shot my load all over the guy's lap, the woman came all over my face. She was a squirter; I could see and feel that. She gushed her wet and horny snatch all over me in huge amounts.

This foursome experience was leaving me fucked hard and hung out to dry I must say. I didn't have much more left in me I didn't think. But I was wrong again. Just when I thought things couldn't get any kinkier, they heated up about ten notches. The woman approached me with about an 8-inch strap on and asked me where I most wanted to get fucked. I told her my pussy. So she laid me down on my side and let me have it. While she did me hard, the two men groped my tits and sucked them hard and vehemently.

After the woman fucked me, she unstrapped the cock and told me to fuck her with it. So I did. She got up on her hands and knees and I did her. It gave me an empowering feeling like nothing I had ever experienced sexually in my entire life! It was liberating and freeing. After all of our crazy sex acts seemed to go over for the time being me and the three others proceeded to lick and suck the remains of the sex we had off of each other. That in itself was an experience highly erotic and nasty. I licked both cocks clean of mine and the other woman's pussy, and it tasted so fucking good it almost made me cum again. The entire experience was amazing and naughty, and something I would definitely do again.

Once again, I felt my eyes trying their hardest to open to the sunlight peeping through my window. I once again woke up uncertain of exactly what had happened to me the night before. But I also felt certain that it would happen to me more. I was sore, fucked hard, had cum running down my legs, and covered with hickies on my neck and tits.

I'll admit I wasn't sure if I had gone completely mad or if my experiences were authentic. My life these days felt like a really nasty episode of the Twilight Zone. I considered during all of these odd experiences to call my erotic writing quits. But the naughty woman and nymphomaniac in me would not hear of it! As I pen this now, I really don't know if my imagination has gone haywire and if I need to see a shrink or if my own lusty and sexually innovative characters have simply cum to life.

4 FUCKED IN HER SLEEP

I was getting down right infuriated. It seemed as though every time I went to the mailbox or even for a small jaunt, the neighbor next door would be whispering or simply looking at me funny.

It was beginning to get very uncomfortable and I was starting to dislike my neighbor, Todd. He was a hot-blooded American man though, and of course, he had the desire to share any juicy piece of gossip he could about a woman. Todd was recently divorced and had some issues, it was true, but I could swear he would look at me like I was his own personal sex slave.

A woman has good intuition and my intuition was telling me something naughty was up with Todd, and it had something to do with me. I just couldn't put my finger on it so to speak. I may not have the best judgment of late anyway, considering the fact I had been suffering with some sleep issues lately. I would wake up every morning feeling very restless and like I hadn't slept at all. It was very tiring and distressing to say the least. When I was asleep, it was kind of like I really wasn't asleep at all. I was asleep and awake at the same time. Kind of like what you hear about near death experiences, how the person looms above the bed and can see their bodies lying on a hospital bed as they are trying to be resuscitated.

I was tired, so I could feel myself drifting off to dream land. I could also see my body nearly floating off of the bed and onto the floor then across my bedroom over to my doorway. I slowly drifted out the door and I swear it looked as though I was headed straight for Todd's house next door. In fact, what I did was go in through his deck gate and I suddenly started undressing right there late at night by Todd's pool. Remember, I was in a sleep state, so there was absolutely nothing I could do about my overly sexed behavior.

I could not believe my eyes, but I swear I started fingering my patch right there in Todd's backyard without a care in the world. I was even letting out some fairly loud sexual moans that would alert the neighbors that I was horny as fuck and going to take my sexual fun and make it myself.

I actually could not believe my eyes. I got up on Todd's diving board (the higher one) and started masturbating quite ferociously. As I was fingering my pussy into nirvana, I noticed Todd was coming towards me on the diving board. I could see that his cock was big and bulging and as hard as cold steel. He came towards me wanking his cock vigorously. I could tell by the look in his smoldering eyes that I was about to have my slit pounded hard.

He came, took my hand, and led me down from the diving board and then he laid me on my tummy on the big chaise lounge and slowly, inch by inch, began to fuck my fiery twat. I cannot describe here how hot it felt to have a blazing hard cock burying itself slowly but surely inch by inch into the gap between your legs. It drove me fucking wild as hell. I loved the first pop inside because I could feel his pulsating ridge gliding and bumping inside of me. It was too fucking hot to be true. I ground on his prick backwards and drove my hot ass harder yet into his steely rod. I wanted this dick every which way but loose, and then some. I flipped over and asked him to take me inside and fuck me up against the wall. He complied. He threw everything off the table and he first took a long Italian cucumber from a basket and began lightly massaging my love button with it. This made my clit stand tall to attention like a small cock.

I was one horny as fuck woman. Then he greased the cucumber down with olive oil and plunged that fucker hard into my swollen love gash. It felt so damn good I winced and let one small squirt go. It felt so hot releasing a bit of my love nectar all over Todd's randy dick. He moaned and I could tell he released a bit of dick spunk at the same time. Todd and I fucked everywhere we could find. He even did me on my knees on the staircase. This is where he finally unloaded what seemed a gallon of spunk in me. I saw myself then get up and head towards the door. I assumed I was headed through the gate and to my house, but I turned left and went towards Todd's next-door neighbor's house. Damn I was some kind of sleepwalking nympho!

The house next door belonged to a single and hot as fuck black dude. I made my way to his door and it just opened up and was not locked. I walked inside and the black hunk was waiting for me by the door. I didn't see him and as I walked past him, he grabbed my arm from behind, swung me around, and kissed me hard, yet tender. His full moist lips were the softest lips ever and made my slit instantly drenched with horny twat cream.

We barely made it to a chair and he had me bent over it, sliding his black dong in and out of me excruciatingly slow. I had never been screwed by a black penis before, (unless I had come over here at night before, and I probably had) and his peter was one of the best I had ever had. This black cock had it going on. He had what I call the 4 H's. He was hot, horny and hung like a horse. For about nine strokes he fucked my horny cunt and then suddenly all 9 inches plunged into my oceanic twat. To tell you the truth, I thought I'd nut right there and not be able to take much more screwing by this dark chocolate morsel from paradise. He definitely knew his way around a pussy. He pulled the throbbing muscle out of my oozing pussy and my cream just literally dripped down the shaft. He looked at his pulsating dick and then looked at me like his sexual wheels were spinning.

He then started inching his black bulge inside my ass. At first I didn't know if I would be able to take the dark rod inside me, but as he inched it in, it filled my ass up totally. It felt so damn good my pussy gushed some cream. He rolled me over, held my legs up, and started to pound my snatch again. Then, just when I thought my snatch would explode, he pulled the wet sticky cock out of me and asked me to suck the fuck out of it. I got on my knees in front of him and went to town on the hungry dick in front of my face. Fuck, it tasted like yummy, juicy dick and I loved it.

I was bound and determined to get his throbbing prick deep inside my throat balls-deep. His dick tasted delicious and seductive. I had never in my life had such a delectable cock deep in my throat. My neighbor was enjoying the carnival of love that was on his cock too, it was easy to tell. He was in sheer and unadulterated ecstasy, no doubt. After I had swallowed him whole for about 10 minutes solid, this nasty man told me he wanted to fuck me harder than I had ever been fucked by a cock before. He suggested that we get in the shower and see what comes up. I knew what would come up! His 9-inch nail gun would.

We scurried to the shower and let our passion get the best of us. He screwed me every which way but loose. It felt so freaking good being hammered by a dick of such huge proportions. I watched on in ecstasy as this dick let my snatch have it and then some. I couldn't believe what an absolute nympho I became when I was asleep. He pinned me to the shower wall and fucked me good. He also turned me around to face him and held my weight as his dick did the nasty to my greedy pussy. I could not get enough of his chocolate covered love pole. After he fucked me until I could hardly walk, he led me to the door. He kissed me goodbye with the most passionate kiss I have ever tasted.

I watched myself head out the door and I assumed I was going back home, but then I saw myself head across the street. I swear I couldn't believe it, but I was going to the Mexican guy's house. He had recently gotten divorced. I was being such a sleepwalking whore! I had seen this guy's cock and it was massive.

He seemed to be expecting me and he opened the door, pulled me in, and proceeded to fuck me right up against the door jam. Damn, his cock wasn't as long as the black dude's, but it was fat and felt good screwing my slash. He plunged his Spanish dick in and out of me hard and furious. Then I got down on my knees and sucked the ever-living fuck out of him. He responded with jolts and jerks of his hot body that made me just want to suck harder and faster.

My pussy has been blinked so many times tonight that it was pulsing a fiery red color that oozed white cream galore. I was a horny bitch that couldn't get enough hot lovin'. But even though I had an inflamed snatch, I simply couldn't get fucked enough. The more of his dick I got, the more I craved. I suddenly decided that I needed to screw his Mexican dick reverse cowgirl style. Of course, he was happy to oblige.

He lay down on the sofa and I mounted his Spanish stallion. I turned with my back to him reverse cowgirl and rode him as hard as I could and as hot and horny as I could. He thrust up into my wanton pussy as I rode his hungry prick. I couldn't fuck enough to satiate my appetite or sexual activities. That is all I wanted to do anymore. You could tell that in my semi-unconscious state I was definitely a nymphomaniac.

After screwing the Mexican 9 ways to Sunday, I headed out the door and back over to the black dude's house again! He opened the door as if to say I knew you'd be back. He led me upstairs to his bedroom where he laid me down, picked my legs up, and put them up by my ears and rammed his 9-inch gun inside of me. I came all over his big black love rod at least twice, and I could tell he was going for three. After getting me to shoot that third time, he went down on my drenched pussy and ate the fuck out of it. It felt so damn good that my body trembled and my legs shook. I could easily tell by my reaction that this big black cock was the one that I, in my sleep induced state, preferred most. It was obvious, since his is the cock I returned to for second helpings. He once again lifted me up against the wall, held my weight, and very expertly thrust his love wand in and out of me in a manner that showed he knew what he was doing and how to handle the 9 inches he had been blessed with. As he screwed my slit like this, his tongue did circles and licks around my very sensitive left areola, sending me to the moon. It seemed as if I would never stop reaching the heights of orgasm. Just as I thought he had made me cum for the last time, I felt my uterus begin the warm contractions again and then send them pulsing through my entire horny body. This man knew how to get my body to writhe in unbelievable ecstasy. I just wished I would remember how hot he was tomorrow. But I never remember these excursions. I just wake up sore and drenched in dick squirt, knowing somehow I've been fucked.

I try hard the next day to put all of the pieces together but I never can. I just notice the stares and the funny looks from these guys. They know that at night I become an insatiable sex fiend. I just wonder if I do more and simply don't know any of it. I can't help but wonder if there are other cocks in the neighborhood I have screwed in my sleep. Maybe I have even done women? I guess until I go to a doctor and tell them what has happened I will never know, but the truth is I don't want to do that because I like getting fucked in my sleep way too much.

5 PEEPING TINA

I yearned to feel his huge bulging cock inside of me, since that day I caught a glimpse of him. I imagined his touch, his kiss, and how he would tease my dripping vagina with his fingertips. It was a year ago; I noticed the door opened to my sister Cybil's bedroom. The melody of passionate sex left Cybil's mouth as Jordan played with his tongue. As I drew close, the smell took possession of my senses, and I found myself itching to see this pleasurable act taking place. Cybil lied there with her eyes closed and back bridged submissively to Jordan's exquisite tongue-lashings. Again and again, I began to develop thoughts of him slowly pulling down my panties and watching me hiss as

I get wetter by his gentle touch. I thought I had gone unnoticed, but Jordan had me already locked in his visual and started sliding his fingers halfway in my sisters throbbing pussy. It was like he was calling the orgasms buried deep in the depths of Cybil's treasure chest. Cybil sighed, “Oh my God,” as his tactic of saying “come here,” inside her had gotten forceful pressing against her G-spot, and as he attempted to slide another finger inside to assist the other. She shouted with joy, squirting love juice all over his face.

My hipsters were soaked as I fought against my hands, wanting to satisfy the urges that now haunt my aching body. I felt the cum running down my legs, awaiting what would soon after follow in this playful stage. Cybil rose up, ripping his boxers off, revealing this huge monster of a cock, instantly causing her mouth to water and crave this wonder dick that she held in her hands. Without hesitation, she put the head inside her awaiting mouth, sliding her tongue around in circles before trying to shove it deeper down her throat.

At that moment, Jordan turned his eyes away from Cybil and gazed deep into my nervous eyes with a smile and a growl of satisfaction as she went deeper down his shaft. I could not contain myself anymore, searching frantically for my saturated gash to please its unrelenting call to be fumbled with. Jordan grabbed her breast pushing her back onto the mattress and pulled her close to the edge into position. His huge love stick pierced her hungry wound as they kissed to manipulate more natural lubrication to form.

With one hand over my mouth, and the other now dancing against my pounding love button, I watched his dick disappear inch for inch for inch. The moisture from my pubic mound brought tears to my eyes, as I grew weary of my fingertips not being enough to curve this seemingly unsatisfiable urge. I staggered to my bedroom desperately in search for heavy artillery to ease this craving between my thighs. I quickly found my double-headed vibrator. With one swift thrust, I shoved this piece of fine craftsmanship deep inside my welcoming gap. Inflamed with lust, my snatch quivered even more with excitement and eagerness.

My thoughts become a cinema of porn as my hips elevated up and down to the roar of this double-headed sex utensil. I found it hard to come back to earth from such arousal; my breathing raced against my heartbeat as the oh-so-short explosive orgasm crept through my uterus beckoning to be freed from the abyss. I began to moan the chants that led to ecstasy as the speed from my vibrator increased, intensifying this orgasmic eruption I had caused. Then with a twitch, I felt a million contractions surge through my body and vagina causing me to release the dam that held my love potion, flowing out like a river onto the bed sheets.

It's Monday, I think, and my name is Tina; I am here to take you on an adventure. You see, some of you have already heard my thoughts from a previous encounter with my sister Cybil and her now husband Jordan whom drove me to the depths of erotic ecstasy with their sexual act. Since then, I have had experience with others, yet none of them as lustful as that first time.

The Omega Ladymatic radiated from my arms with the scent of Ralph Lauren Romance to tickle the attraction of the opposite sex. My beast was contained as I desperately pursued to escape this city, bound by the journey to find pleasure, because I knew what I've had until now wasn't enough.

As I walked down the open streets of the outskirts of neighboring towns and villages, like a ferocious lion to prey on victims, the air began to shift, changing my mood, and increasing my titillating senses even more.

This evening's summer heat, alleviated

by the fresh salt-filled breeze, traversed across the still ocean waves, bestowing in my hair and clothes a fresh oceanic scent. Passion gripped me firmly with his teeth, clenching onto me as if he had a mission to use me as his target.

Fate took over this jagged course leading me along the rolling hills of curves of the land displayed in an array of dark greens and floral on its vast countryside. The pale crimson sky and crescent moon became a silent guide as once again this overwhelming feeling came that I just could not suppress. My thoughts are filled with a kaleidoscope of rouge-ish emotions that serve my unbearable lust. I feel as if I could soon burst from the excitement and waves of sexual frustration that plague my body once more. I immediately scrambled to find a bus and shelter that led me closer to the ocean's floor. However, my legs are shaking, and I have begun to rock against the gentle soft-cushioned seats.

"What do I do?" The bumps in the road intensify the unsuspected thrashing of my passion. Not to give myself off as obvious to what was taking place, I arch my back a little and lean my head back in an obsessed wicked trance. The bus came to a stop. Hurrying off, I grimaced as the convulsions distracted me from the fresh-scented ocean breeze. Punished by this present dilemma, I found myself in a hopeless situation. I failed to keep my pelvic muscles squeezed, and the honey dew from my pussy ran down my legs.

I felt my body inhibit shudders of ecstasy that was dominating more than my mere thoughts, but my entire sense of composure.

I soon came upon the secure confines of a public restroom and ran desperately towards the entrance. Here, I knew I was free to seek out this itch buried between my knees. I noticed the overly clean restroom was clear of visitors as I frantically made my way to a cubicle and began to free my eagerly inviting beaver. Suddenly, a loud commotion broke my concentration for just a moment. A couple had the same idea of getting a quick fix, tearing through the door of the bathroom stall next to mine. I drew my attention slowly through a hole that I quickly and conveniently took courtesy of. Casting my sights upon the burning hot second pair of love lips the young girl presented oh so freely, I can feel my clit jumping and beckoning to make contact with my small portable vibrator. I watched quietly as the young well-hung man did his clit massage of counter clockwise circles around this young vixen's love button.

As if an orgasm was programmed from each stroke of his tongue, multiple orgasms caused my beautiful aroused jewel to ooze even more. I can feel my stomach began to cramp into a small knot at the fear that my serenity would soon break.

My plea goes unheard inside my head as I am trembling for the self-pleasuring ritual my longing twat wants to partake in. I found it hard to swallow the saliva that drooled from my lips as I watched speechless, leading my own orgasms to implode. I try to pull myself together and hold out but this hunger to release has so much tension, I can't hold it any longer.

"Mmmmm." Shit, I cover my mouth quickly as the next one comes faster than the first. At that moment, the young couple next to me switch positions so that the young man could glide nicely into her hot steaming vagina. The vein in his cock had grown from the rush of blood flowing through his shaft.

As he prepared to enter her love gash, she stopped him and said, "No Baby, let me guide you."

She took his nicely endowed manhood and stuffed it slowly into her tight swollen asshole. It seemed as if it wouldn't fit, but she maneuvered her body back onto his pole, swallowing its size inch for inch. As her glory hole loosened, she began to cum a third and fourth time. The anal play was so overwhelmingly hot for its young intruder that after the third minute he had reached his climax. Removing his cock as fast as possible, the young woman turned and inhaled his cream down her waiting throat. I found this lovely act of animalism hot as fuck. I immediately had the urge to satisfy my own sexual urges.

After they had cleaned themselves up, I finally pulled myself together because I was unable to completely satisfy the tickling between my thighs. I had to find a hotel. The darkness had become thick, and though I was yearning to be fucked, I didn't want it to be taken so freely. Finding a hotel close to the restrooms, I checked in and took a shower. It had gotten chilly earlier, and I had the perfect opportunity to wear my trench coat. The red and black sexy outfit fit perfectly, and I was soon on my way. Reaching the lobby, I found that they had computers openly available for their guests. I then went on to search for nightlife in this small rural town. It just so happens as I was searching I came across an old friend that is a very attractive black man that I had met earlier in a bad marriage.

Des was 5'11 and built like a tank. Huge arms, very broad shoulders, and a heart made of gold. Honestly, I have never had a relationship with a black man before, but I knew he could be the one. I saw him online writing, and as usual, I had to flirt. It was uncontrollable with him and his womanizing charm. I made arrangements to meet him finally at the train station around 10 pm. Because I knew he was in love with my long silky red hair and nicely shaped breasts, I hurried up stairs and took off the outfit I had on and redressed myself. This time, I was intending on showing him what I was made of and wore nothing underneath the long trench coat. As I arrived at the train station, I saw him standing there with a single rose, and without saying a word, he pulled me to him and kissed me long, deep, and passionately.

The feeling that I had finally gotten control of earlier immediately shot through my pussy again as if it had never left. I was afraid that he might be like the black guys I was warned about my whole life, but in just the blink of an eye, he had erased the racial differences that were drilled inside my head since childhood.

He asked, "Tina what do you want to do this evening? Are you hungry, or do you want to go have a glass of wine, or coffee?" My mind was still stuck on his kiss, and my body was well beyond giving me signals to go home with him.

Squirming in the car's leather seat sticking to my legs I uttered, "Can we actually go somewhere where we can talk a little and get to know each other?"

He instantly replied. "Of course, let's go

to my house, unless you want to go somewhere else, which I am perfectly ok with."

So after an agreement to return to his place, we soon came upon this huge apartment building with elevators almost more luxurious as my hotel. He led me down the long corridor to a door in the middle of the entire floor and opened it slowly. What seemed to be a small normal-sized bachelor pad became a penthouse meant for pleasure.

He explained to me that the entire floor belonged to him, so I should feel comfortable to do whatever I would like. We talked briefly before I suggested that we take a shower together. His eyes sparkled like stars, and his stare was so intense that I felt chills come all over me, rendering goose bumps. He led me to the biggest of three bathrooms in the house, and I then stopped him and made him wait as I prepared.

"Can I take your coat?" he asked.

He was mesmerized by my beauty and made me feel wonderfully sexy. As he went to leave, I said, "Look closely at what I want to give you!" and then gave him my coat.

Respectfully, he went outside and

awaited my signal for him to join me. Impatiently, I sent the invite, excited with lust and impelled sensual desire to feel him in me. He revealed his 9-inch cock by dropping his boxers to the steaming hot bathroom floor and pushing the glass door between us open.

I turned, leaning my head against the shower wall, and awaited his masculine touch, only to find him dazed by what he saw. The heat of the water and smell of his shower gel didn't contribute anything to alleviate this consuming pain of pleasurable desire. I watched as the beaded drops of water pearled down his chocolate skin, and he pressed his long hard monster against my 5-foot tall body. One arm was pulling me close, caressing my left breast. He then began to dry me off with his tongue, trailed by kisses, as I held my head back against his chest. Snuggled close to me from behind, he attacked my beautiful breasts first, his grip so firm, massaging his way down and then back up the tight curves of my body.

His hand then massaged up to my nipples that instantly became erect and rock hard, playing with them so tenderly that I began to moan. Standing on my tiptoes, I pressed my small round ass against his abdomen and rubbed against his enormous hard penis. Lightning flashed through my body as his penis swelled to full hardness and straightened up. I did a provocative booty cheek spread as he laid his 9-inch rod up between them. He rubbed my back as I was savoring the feeling that my firm breasts were in his hands. I began to breathe more heavily now as he made this feeling of excitement grow more intense.

He turned me around, elevating one of my feet, massaging and kissing my calves from ankles upward, moving to my buttocks until he had reached my stomach. After going to his knees, he plunged between my crisp, plump cheeks and soaped my sweet grooves. The appeal made me shudder in his hands. He was playing with the fire that ignited my pleasure. His fingers played between my tender cheeks, gently massaging my anus, moving towards my pussy. He feverishly lashed his tongue through my pussy. With two fingers, he gently glided over the rosette of my sensitive skin, stretching my skin only a little. He had created just a thrill, a hot feeling, and then, he took it away.

In return, the fingers of his other hand began to move now on my hills streaked down so gently on my labia, over my perineum, until he had reached my anus again. This time, he slipped his tongue into the back entrance of my innocence and drilled it inside, pulling my buttocks apart and into his tongue. He tongue fucked my asshole, taking advantage of the distraction of my climax.

He then rose up and lowered my body down, while our mouths met and our tongues began to devour each other. His hands kneaded my beautiful breasts lightly, caressing the solid curves, and then slowly and suddenly his hard gorgeous cock slid into my hot tight pussy. His penis had taken the entrance to paradise, the noticeable vibration was transmitted throughout my body and the incredible narrowness made the deeper penetration very difficult.

Now, he started pushing apart my red-hot tight pussy while kneading my ass, massaging my anus; he pushed his middle finger into my asshole. Slowly sliding deeper and deeper, I could feel his fingers only separated by a thin membrane at the bottom of my flask.

I yelled, "Yes... yes... oh... mmmh" and came toward him more. Our movements took on momentum, until a long-drawn cry of climax reached and collapsed on me. He held back while enjoying the twitching of my body, and I enjoyed it as well. My muscles tensed around his shaft; I savored to the fullest the feel of him inside me, as I slowly calmed down and then looked at him with a dreamy smile. I love it and the look in my new partner's eyes when he caresses me this way.

6 DOMINATRIX DIVA

I am a dominatrix and a damn good one if I do say so myself. I work hard for my money, but I don't put up with any bullshit. When I do my job, I am in charge and that's just the way it is. If my clients don't like it, they can find another dominatrix.

I loved making my clients beg and plead, crawling on their hands and knees to be serviced and pleased sexually. I knew my job well and I always came well equipped with the proper toys and devices. My clients loved collars, chains, vibes, cattle prods, and whips, just to name a few. If they needed a spanking, I was happy to do so, and if they wanted spanked and teased and blindfolded, then all the better. When I was at work, I was their mistress, and they better damn well do what I say or else. I didn't necessarily fuck and suck them. I only fucked if I felt like it. I am not a hooker.

I headed out to the door on the way to my first client of the day. He was a 55-year-old and kinky as hell. I had my whole diva attire on. I had on a black leather bustier, red fishnet stockings, and black stiletto come-fuck-me boots, and I had my bag packed with all of my goodies in it. This was going to be a thrilling afternoon getting paid big bucks to push this guy around.

I arrived at his house and he opened the door with a big ol' goofy grin on his face. He was a chubby dude and bald. But man did he like to be treated like shit. Right off the bat, I commanded that he get his ass down on the ground. Then I put my come-fuck-me boot heel into his back and told him to start begging. He did as I said and begged his mistress to whip him hard with her leather strap, and I thrashed my awaiting whip on his pale white skin. I gave him about ten good lashes just to make his ass sting and turn bright pink. I then cuffed his hands and gave him a good kick before I demanded him to stand up.

Now it was time to make this guy my pet. I had left him a note in his bedroom, so I commanded him to go in there and read and do as it said. I told him to knock on the bedroom door like a good boy when he was through reading the note. He did as I said and I went into the bedroom at that time, uncuffed him, and then tied his hands with rope.

I had my paddler in my hand just in case my pet got out of line. He sometimes would act out to get a good swat on his white ass. He did so at this time. He started whining like a baby. I yelled, "Get down boy!"

He went to his knees and then stuck his ass high up in the air. I took my paddle and swatted the fuck out of him five times.

Now it was time to blindfold my little pet. I commanded him to stand back up. He said, "Yes, Miss," and stood the fuck up.

I stroked his head two times for obeying my command, but no more. He didn't deserve many rewards yet. It was also an order that no client of mine would have an orgasm unless I said they could!

Now it was time to take my man toy into the shower and drive him fucking crazy with desire. I had it all prepared ahead of time. For this delicious slave treat, we stripped down to our birthday suits. I have an electric shaver that I took in the shower with us so that I could shave every bit of hair off of his balls and groin area. I told him to hold his arms high in the air as I shaved his balls closely, making sure to fondle them just enough to drive him out of his mind with longing. I noticed that his big fat cock was getting hard as steel while I did my work on him. Then I commanded that he turned around, and I whipped his wet soapy ass with ten good slaps until it turned pink as a ripe nipple.

I loved spanking his shiny, wet, hungry ass until he begged me to stop or to keep going, and that is exactly what I did over and over again. Then I turned my pet around and rubbed my hard 36DD tits all over him, not allowing him one touch of my sexy body. Then I demanded my man toy to get out of the shower and do as his mistress told him to or I would give him five lashes with my whip.

After the hot shower, I was in the mood to have my snatch eaten out and eaten out good. So I commanded that he shave his face impeccably, not leaving one bit of stubble, or he could not have one bite of my wet peach. Then I harshly told him to kneel down on his knees and eat my perfectly clean pussy. I was bound and determined to get some sexual satisfaction out of this deal.

I allowed him to finger me with his big, hard thumb, but he was not allowed to touch his seething cock or to cum, or I would give him hard lashes. He ate my pussy out so hard and so good that I came all over my slave's face. I didn't let him clean my cum off of his face. I made him smell it and wish he could fuck my pussy for a while longer. Then I told my slave to go into the other room.

In the other room, I had a camera set up and I commanded my love slave to do an erotic dance for me. I tossed him a cock ring and demanded that he put it on at that moment or I'd paddle his buttocks until they turned red. He quickly put the ring on as I ordered and behaved like the perfect slave. I also had brought a dick pump along with me for extra playtime activities and added fun.

I watched on as he pumped away at his throbbing member. The head was bulging so big I must admit my mouth was watering to get around that hot cock. To drive him even more insane with desire, I began to finger the fuck out of my snatch while he watched on with his mouth near watering by now. I knew my pussy was absolutely irresistible for this slave of mine.

I decided it was time for me and my slave to have a bit of role-play fun. I told him to go look in his bedside table drawer and there he would find a note. Of course, he did as I commanded and went into his bedroom where he found a note that said this:

I will be your own private audience

tonight in my chambers at the Royal Bath House. You should know that I have decided to send our troops into battle, and there is nothing you can do to persuade me not to, my dear warrior. See that no one you know comes with you or I will deny access to you as well.

My slave emerged from his bedroom ready and willing to participate in everything I ordered him to do. I made sure my slave knew that if he dared to touch me anywhere on my body, he would be arrested and killed on the spot. I made sure that as I spoke these words to him, I undressed very seductively, so much so that I swear he drooled looking at all of my beautiful girly bits. I could see in his face that he wanted to grab his dick and jerk off so bad from looking at my shaved and slick pussy.

I finally allowed him to stick one knee out to me so I could grind my aching wet pussy on it, but he still was not allowed to touch. I had my paddle handy just in case he got obstinate. I told him to bend over and I paddled his pink ass, then I commanded him to stand up. This is when I put clothespins on his nipples so they could be pinched while he stuck his knee back out and I ground some more on it.

I decided he had been a good boy so I allowed him to go back down on my pussy one more time for only five minutes. I admit my hungry slit was aching and hurting to squirt all over his smoothly shaven face, but I knew if I did that, he'd cum all over the place and he wasn't allowed to have an orgasm this session.

I commanded my boy toy to go sit down across the room like a good slave and pump his dick up some more. I wanted his dick so big it would nearly burst out of the pump. As he pumped away at his hurting muscle, I made him watch on as I went after my snatch with my rabbit vibrator. I went to town on my pussy full throttle. It was easy to see that I had done this before. I went after my pussy hole expertly and diligently.

After I came in front of him, I gave him the choice of either getting himself off or paying me and then I leave. Of course, he jerked the fuck out of himself and squirted nearly across the room. I collected my pay, got dressed, and went home to have a bite to eat before my next client.

My next client was a lesbian woman. She really liked to get kinky so I had to get all of my supplies handy. With my lesbian client, it's all about making her submit, but I still feed her sexual appetite at the same time. I knocked on her door and she anxiously let me in. She appeared ready, willing, and horny as fuck.

I immediately went to work. I removed my trench coat to reveal the full attire of a dominatrix diva underneath. I looked up at my client to see her put her hand to her pussy, very obviously turned on already by my domineering appearance. I reached inside my bag and got out the metal cuffs. If she was so easily going to start fingering her cunt, I needed to restrain her as quickly as possible.

I very easily led her on, making her believe she would have full access to my beautiful bits and more. I gave my cunt a few finger plunges and my clit a few tickles. I then lifted up my ample left tit and gave my hard nipples a suck and a few laps of my tongue. I decided today to drive my female girl slave a bit nuts. I would do the start-and-stop dominatrix routine that usually drove her up the wall and sent her into an orgasmic frenzy. If she got out of line trying to insist I finish her cunt off, I would give her clit a few taps with my spanker. That teaches her to back off and do what her master tells her to do. She was one nasty bitch and I had to handle her with big girl gloves. After teasing her for several minutes, this is when I always take it up a notch. I looked my girl toy in the face very intensely and demanded that she listen and listen well. I told her by no means is she to cum or there will be hell to pay.

Eventually my lesbo girl toy went completely berserk and couldn't hold her cum any longer. She started to squirt all over the carpet. I decided to surprise her and I commanded her to lie down while I finished her wet snatch up. I buried my head between her mocha thighs and went to town on her pussy that was hot pink on the inside. She writhed and squirmed as I wallowed deep inside her dark pussy. She jerked a few times and her legs began to tremble. I knew that meant a full body orgasm was right around the corner.

As she started to squirt all in my mouth, I took my paddle and swatted her ass at the same time. As she lifted her ass up off the ground, I'd give it a sharp swat, too. That simply made her cum harder and longer. She groped and clawed the carpeting with her fingernails. She was lying in the same spot that she had "accidentally" come in earlier.

Suddenly I jumped up and quit eating the fuck out of her horny cunt. Then I told her to stay put and not to move. She was furious but turned the fuck on all at the same time. I stood up just out of her reach so she couldn't touch me while I jerked my clit off hard and vigorously. I was wearing a pair of hot black leather pants with the crotch cut out of them. It was perfect for my nasty clit to show through. I fingered my clit so hard you could hardly see my fingers moving. It felt hotter than fuck and I knew I was about to gush everywhere.

I could hardly stand up; it was going to be so damn intense. It gave me pleasure looking at my slave girl's face wanting to get her mouth and hands all over my nasty snatch. I smiled very naughtily at her, making her start begging and whining like a pup wanting this pussy. But no way would she get it. I then released my index finger off of my clit and let the river flow. I gushed all over her carpeting, wetting everything down in sight. I writhed, screamed, and sucked my left tit ferociously while I gushed out white cream. It ran down my leg and I walked within licking distance of my concubine. But I did not allow her a single lick. In fact, I took my fingers and got some of my own cum off of my leg, and then I very sexily licked it off one finger at a time, making her squirt again.

I then cleaned the rest of my cum off of my leg, put on my trench, and commanded that she get up off of the floor. I took the key and unlocked her metal restraints. I ordered her to clean every bit of the mess, and she did so like a good little pet. I then asked for my pay, took my check, and headed out to the door. Boy was I tired. I headed home towards my loft and thought this sure is a nasty job, but hey, somebody's got to do it. I laughed to myself, headed upstairs, and laid down for a good afternoon nap.

7 THE GARDENER SEES ALL

I was a gardener by trade and I did the lawns for many well-to-do people across the city of Los Angeles. It isn't the easiest profession in the world, but it pays the bills, so I'm not complaining. After the day I was about to have unbeknownst to me, I definitely wouldn't be complaining.

I drove into the driveway of a very rich couple that had a massive lawn. I was always sure to put aside a whole day for their garden work. They had tons of rose bushes and other bushes as well to tend. Also, they had at least 10 trees to feed and prune. I also took care of their vegetable garden.

I got out of my truck and started to unload my tools. I knew I was in for a long, hard day, and when I said hard, I didn't realize just how ironic that statement was. But that's okay as I can handle anything anyone wants to throw at me usually.

The people that lived here are extremely rich and I waved them off as I saw them both pull out in their driveway in their matching Mercedes Benz'. I got my stuff together and headed for the massive back yard to do some pruning of the bushes. I got out my pruning shears and started working diligently. As I was working hard and starting to build up some sweat, I noticed something out of the corner of my eye. I noticed that my client's beautiful college-aged daughter was sunbathing by the pool.

Man, she was a hot senorita. I noticed she glanced over at me and she could see I was watching her with my tongue wagging and I also appeared to be drooling. She kind of snickered and smiled very seductively at me. Damn, the things me and that girl could do!

She was about 5 feet, 4 inches tall with a gorgeous golden suntan. She had long, straight golden brown hair to match her gorgeous body. Her eyes were an emerald green that sparkled in the sun. I had seen her up close and personal before and knew what her beautiful face looked like.

She was hotter than hot and just the

type of girl that makes my cock swell. In fact, as I watched her writhe around on her chaise lounge, my cock was getting huge. She undid her bikini top, and lo and behold, she exposed her plump, ripe nipples to me. I almost busted a nut right then and there.

Damn she looked hot as fuck. I watched as she rubbed oil all over those ripe nipples, and my boner was starting to hurt by this time. I went behind one of the butterfly bushes and gave my dick a few strokes before I came all over myself. It felt good rubbing my hands all over the greedy head of my cock. I could feel the precum and I took my thumb and rubbed all over my swollen dick head.

I knew I better get back to work so I zipped up and emerged from the bush. I mean no pun by that statement of course. When I got back to work feeding and pruning trees, I could not believe my eyes! The hot little college cutie was skinny dipping - in the shallow pool nonetheless. She looked so fucking foxy frolicking around. Then she laid a towel out right by the edge and damn if she didn't start fingering her twat. Her cunt wasn't either hairy or completely bald. She had a blondish to light brown landing strip that looked sexy as fuck. I could only imagine how sweet that nasty peach tasted. Of course, I mean nasty in the sexual sense.

It looked sparkling clean with the sunrays bouncing off of it.

What made this whole scenario so damn hot was the fact that she knew I was watching. That just added to the appeal. This girl was too much and way too hot to handle. She was trying real hard to turn me the fuck on so I couldn't get any work done. I was old enough to realize exactly what she was up to.

Even though she played innocent, this nasty girl knew exactly what she was doing. I could tell she had seduced older men before. She was just tempting me to come inside that gate and fuck her brains out right there by the water.

I knew better than to do that though if I wanted to keep my clients happy and keep my checkbook happy as well. But I couldn't help but wank on my prick some more while I watched her finger the fuck out of herself. I tried to stop watching her but she just kept turning it up a notch. I couldn't peel myself away from her for nothing. She was too tantalizing and way too fucking hot.

It now appeared that she was reaching in her bag for her heavy artillery. When her hand emerged, it came out with a purple vibrating 'bi-cock.' This hot tamale then stood up and began to do a little striptease for me and my hot dick.

She looked over at me very seductively

and my cock stood up in attention. This girl was going to make me nuts in 2 minutes if she kept this up. Her body was absolutely amazing. I could not find one flaw on her beautiful frame. Her legs were slender and golden and the water on them looked hot glistening in the sun. Her tits were perfect, plump C cups with naughty ripe nipples that I wanted to suckle so bad my prick hurt.

I longed to slip inside her seething vagina with the sexy landing strip. She spread her tanned thighs wide open and let me see a bird's eye view of her dripping cunt. It looked good enough to eat and way more. Then she went to town on it with her heavy artillery. She stroked her cunt hard with that 8-inch vibrator. She squirmed and moaned while she did so, and it drove me near to the brink of orgasm. I had to sneak off to the tool shed just to let my dick get out for a while and release a bit of precum before this cock of mine exploded all over my stomach and down my legs. It felt amazingly good and horny as hell rubbing the glistening precum all over the fat and bulging head of my meat. I could hardly curtail the massive squirt that was easing up my shaft and trying to emerge right here in this tool shed. This bathing babe had me wanting to screw her brains out and do it so good she'd be sore for a week. I would bang this babe so hard she'd ache every time she walked. It would be obvious to those around her she had been fucked long and hard.

I finally smashed my dick back in my pants and managed to walk back out to the lawn and try to get some work done. I was clipping away at some bushes when I happened to glance over and see the bathing beauty lying out under a tree buck-naked. Then she did something that was super fucking horny. She had a water bottle and she sat down on it real slow little by little. It was hot as hell watching her fuck this plastic cock.

It looked as though she was enjoying the grooves as they slid up and down and in and out of her hungry cunt. Her hot pink lips wrapped around the bottle rather seductively, making me swell to huge proportions just by looking. I could hardly stand the constant ache that was coursing through every vein of my swollen member right now. It pressed uncomfortably against my pants, making it hurt so bad I thought I'd bust 10 nuts in a row.

Miss Get Me Hard continued her bottle extravaganza much to my pleasure and my dismay. She looked over at me as if to tempt me and to see just how I would react to her beautiful cunt that, at this point, was playing all kinds of erotic mind games on this gardener. Fuck! This girl was too much! Was she trying to get me fired or have me sent to an asylum for the sexually insane? But I could not control my animal needs and raw lust. In other words, as long as she was performing this wicked show, I was going to be first in line for proverbial tickets.

It was absolutely fucking time for me to pay another little visit to the trusty tool shed to gather a few implements and to relieve some penile pressure for lack of a better term. I barely made it in the shed before my cock was bounding full speed out of my zipper. I didn't even bother to undo my belt. I unzipped and started wanking.

I was getting with it and not even paying attention, but suddenly it felt as if a pair of eyes was on me. I sheepishly looked towards the little window on the shed and saw her pair of eyes staring inside the tool shed. When she saw that I saw her, she quickly ducked down. I smiled and chuckled to myself and really started giving it to my wanton cock. I put on a show like a stripper diva. I jerked and then I seductively moaned, knowing the college cutie was taking all of this in. Two could play this little temptation game of cat and mouse.

I put on the best show this girl had probably ever seen in her life. I hope it forced her to play with her pussy vehemently and seductively. The thought that she was watching me only increased my interest in this whole sexy afternoon of adult play. It was incredibly exciting to think that a woman enjoyed watching you when you jacked your dick off. This was definitely a first for me. It was usually the other way around. It truly made me feel like I had a 10-inch cock as big around as a soda can.

I was bound and determined not to shoot off all the way but just to allow one good squirt to emerge from the eye on my bulbous dick head. I was going to try to aim it for the window. I knew my little hottie would be out there fingering off and observing closely. I jerked faster and faster still until I felt that first wad rising through my veined shaft. I knew it would be a shot like no other. I just hoped that I could stop there.

As I performed fevered yet slow strokes of my prick shaft, I would also do a little expert work with my thumb around the ridge on the upstroke. It felt so good I almost started trembling all over my body. If this kept up, I would have to sit down. I planted my ass on a stool right in front of the window of the shed. I could see the top of her head; she would duck down when she thought I wasn't looking. It was kind of cute how she tried to hide the fact she was watching me. Suddenly I felt the juicy spunk start to come out from my penis head. It was a one long shot that made a splatter on the window. I made sure to stand up just as I saw it ready to land on the pane. Wow, I could not believe I was able to get a cum shot to travel that distance. After I knew that the load was over, I quickly squeezed my balls and put my dick between my legs like a dog to hold it down and keep it from unloading totally. It wasn't easy to do either. I looked out the window, expecting the college fox to be jerking on her clit, but then I heard the door open behind me.

I looked behind me and it was her; she looked intently at me and said, "Fuck me now." Of course, I was going to fuck her so I immediately pulled her body into mine and gave her a hot, wet, and very passionate kiss. Then I backed her ass up to the wall, lifted her up to my lap level, and banged her hard and steady with my raging cock. She threw her head back and let out a sexy moan that made me screw her all the more vehemently. I wanted to unload my spunk to her back pussy wall and I was just about to do that.

I felt my dick balls draw tighter, and my cock throbbed so damn hard I almost let out a rebel yell myself. She scratched her claws down my back, and I grabbed her long hair and held it in a ponytail, ready to soak the inside of her box down. Suddenly the two of us unleashed the animal within and started to squirt and cream at the same time; she thrashed and I groaned so loud it was possible we were heard by the neighbors. But at that moment, me and my little mermaid didn't care. At that moment, we connected lustfully and very sexually. It was the best fuck I have ever had. After she had her brains screwed out and her box pounded, she quietly satiated her cute little ass out to the yard and I put my clothes back on and finished pruning. She and I never fucked again nor did we speak of our day in the sun. But I'll always remember her. I kind of liked my job. After all, the gardener always sees all.

8 THE HORNY CLASSMATE

My name is Bridgette, and I am enjoying the hell out of my freshman year in college so far. Who knew college could be so fun?

I probably need to explain. As I said, I'm Bridgette and I am very horny all the time. I don't mean "kind of" horny or semi-horny. I mean extremely, super horny. I guess you can call me a nymphomaniac. I looked up the definition of nymphomaniac when I was 18 years old. I decided then and there they should have plastered my picture beside the definition in the dictionary. I love sex and cannot get enough of it. I could get fucked, sucked, or even fingered 24/7, and it still wouldn't be enough to quench my lusty desires.

I am hot as fire and flames, and I have

been ever since I could remember that I had a cunt between my legs. All through my early years, I would get extremely horny in class. I especially got turned on in those classes that were a challenge academically. I would get very hot in the classes with male teachers, of course, especially those who were big and tall, and I could tell they had a big, hard dick in their pants. They got hard as wood when I stood close to them asking a question with my cleavage hanging in their face.

I know that this one particular instructor was attracted to me. I could tell by the look in his eyes. He looked at me with a longing in his eyes that told me he wanted me really bad. During test time, I would get extremely turned on because of the adrenaline coursing through my body. I would sit on my foot and grind my pussy on it and get turned on. Usually, I would come, too. I would try my very best to contain my moans and not let other people know I was having an

It was a thrill wondering if the boys were getting hard-ons and if the girls were getting wet pussies. The thought of the other students getting turned on just made me hornier and made me cum quicker. This may sound really naughty, but like I said, I am a nymphomaniac and have been since I was 14 – maybe even younger than that. I simply could not get enough sex. Even if I had to have it with myself, it didn't matter as long as it was giving me sexual satisfaction. I was happy for a little while, anyway.

I never stayed sexually satisfied for long. I always needed more and more sex. It is kind of like an addiction for me. It always has been and it always will be. I don't think I have ever been totally satisfied sexually. When I arrived at college, I was hoping to encounter more sexual experiences than I ever had before. That was my goal, my plan. I was pleasantly surprised when I found out that was definitely the case. The instructors at college were even hotter. They made my pussy so wet I thought I might explode and gush on the spot.

My favorite instructor was Mr. Williams, my college algebra teacher. He was big, black, and handsome as hell. He was hung well, too. I could see his big, black dick move around in his trousers as he taught us. He was about 6-foot-2 and built like a fucking brick house. I would stare at him as he taught us and just imagine his big, black cock inside me. I could hardly contain my hands in class when I started thinking about me and Mr. Williams doing the mattress mambo. The thought of it was almost too hot to handle. He was all that and a bag of chips, as the saying goes.

I was almost positive that Mr. Williams noticed and desired me, too. You could tell by the sultry look in his eyes. When he leaned over my desk to help me with an algebraic equation, it was easy to see he was looking at my cleavage. Also, I never wear panties, so I tried to give him a sneak peek of my pussy lips when the chance occurred. I could almost hear Mr. Williams groan under his breath when he caught a glimpse of my ivory pussy with its long, hanging pink lips.

I could feel the sexual tension growing between him and me. It was so naughty and erotic. I could see when he grew an instant boner in his pants. I knew right then and there that Mr. Williams wanted me, and he wanted me in a big way. I wanted to fuck and suck him, too. I absolutely couldn't help myself. This big black dude was fucking hot!

I remember the day when Mr. Williams passed out our first algebra test. I was hornier than I had ever been, looking at his big, bulging dick in his pants. He walked around the room passing out the test papers. I could swear when he got to me, he had a devious yet sexual look in his eyes. I was almost certain he wanted me as badly as I did him. We started our test on quadratic equations with word problems. These were extremely hard for me and stressed me out.

As I got more and more frustrated, I noticed my snatch getting extremely wet. I couldn't help but writhe around on my foot and rub my cunt all over it the hornier I got. I knew if my adrenaline level got any higher, I would probably have a spontaneous orgasm right there. The harder the test got, the hornier I got. I was having a hard time containing my moans, too.

I wondered if Mr. Williams or the other students noticed that I was wiggling around in my chair. I also wondered if they knew how close I was to squirting off right in my seat. I was dangerously close. You could practically smell my pussy wafting across the classroom. I was getting more turned on by the minute and having a very difficult time focusing on math problems.

Mr. Williams looked over at me with an intriguing look in his eyes. It's like deep down he knew I was up to something extremely naughty and taboo. I wondered if he knew just how kinky I was. I opened my legs a little bit and flashed him my wet pussy. I know he saw it because he inadvertently touched his dick on the outside of his trousers and then he pulled his hand away quickly as if hoping no one saw him do it.

By this time, I was beside myself and close to the very edge of a hot orgasm. I squirmed harder around on my foot. I looked over at a male student and saw him pulling his cock through his pants. I could tell he was totally turned on and hornier as hell. I wondered if he'd cum right along with me. When I arrived at the final word question, I felt my orgasm coming. I knew it was going to be a good one. Then it started flooding my entire nympho body. It felt so hot as it pierced and flooded my entire being. I tried so damn hard not to make it obvious I was shooting off, but also I kind of wanted people to think I was. Is that naughty or what?

I saw Mr. Williams go and sit down at his desk. By the motion of his upper arm, I could almost swear he was rubbing his dick under his desk. Just thinking it drove me to my orgasm finally. It was one of the best I had ever had. Knowing that I was in a room full of people while I had it didn't hurt the hotness level of it either. It increased it tenfold.

When Mr. Williams walked around the classroom to pick up our test papers, I swear I could feel his hard cock graze my shoulder. He also very quickly slipped a note in my lap. I was so excited I almost squirted in my chair again. I did reach down and give my kitten a few rubs and a quick fondle.

When the students within close proximity of me had cleared the area, I took a peek at his note. All that it said was, “I can smell your snatch and I want to eat the fuck out of it.” I almost blushed. I was too much of a horny little bitch to blush. I simply looked up at him and licked my lips. I then swung my feet around and made sure he got a gaping view of my slit. He would see my quivering quim and my hard clit poking out from between my creamy lips. I would make sure I’d get an A even if I had to suck his cock for hours.

I be-bopped my cute little ass past Mr. Williams and winked at him as I left the classroom. Of course, I made sure to “drop” my own little note on the floor by his desk. I smiled and did a proverbial wave and was pleased that I had teased this big, dark dick so deviantly yet deliciously. I could picture Mr. Williams now as he opened the note and read this: “I crave your big, black pole inside my wet, bald pussy.”

I could almost feel his cock in my hand...stroking it...pulling on it slowly...looking into his eyes with a look that showed how I craved his cock buried in my throbbing cunt. If he only knew how my tight pussy could strangle his cock.

But he would know soon enough...he would truly know.

I couldn't wait for my next algebra class on Wednesday. I planned on an all-out seduction of Mr. Williams. That night as I lay in bed thinking about it, my hands started to play with my pussy lips. I couldn't keep my fingers off of it. I hoped my roommate didn't hear me fingering myself, but she probably did every night anyway. In fact, I could swear some nights she joined me in getting off by masturbating herself.

I was so excited thinking about how I came all over my seat during the algebra test my pussy got drenched almost instantly. I was getting closer than ever to an amazing orgasm now. I started to arch my body off of my mattress. I had to be as quiet as I could so as not to wake my nerdy roommate, who had no respect for the life of a nympho. It was a hard and wet job, but somebody had to do it. I was thinking of Mr. Williams and his big, long, chocolate love pole while I fingered and fisted my cunt. I had always wanted to get myself off by fisting, and tonight I was bound and determined to do it. I almost had all five fingers inside my pussy. It felt fucking hot being wrist deep inside my cunt. I was drenching my entire hand with cunt cream. I imagined how Mr. Williams' dick looked in his tan trousers and how his head made an impression that allowed me to see the outline of it. It made me so wet that I knew I was in for another trip to the laundry with my bed linens. I'm sure everyone thought I peed in my bed or something. Actually, sometimes I would pee at the same time I squirted. I couldn't help my nympho pussy. It just worked that way. When I came, everything liquid would try to escape.

Just thinking about it made me start cumming, and boy did I ever cream good. In fact, I came so good that I made my nerdy roommate finger her cunt off, too. We came together and it was actually kind of hot. I thought maybe the next night I might go down on her pussy and eat it out good.

The next day I made it to algebra 30 minutes early in hopes of catching Mr. Williams. I did. He was at his desk grading papers. I walked over and smiled at him. He looked up at me and gave me a devilish grin like he wanted to fuck my brains out. He calmly walked over to the classroom door and shut and locked it.

I was getting so excited I could feel my pussy leak down my thighs a bit. Before I knew it, he was all the fuck over me. He grabbed the back of my hair and twisted it in his palm. He then started kissing me greedily with his mouth and hot tongue. He reached in my shirt and yanked out my right tit. I was getting drenched by this time. He pressed his big black body next to mine, and I felt his boner raging underneath his pants.

I reached down as he sucked the fuck out of my tits and unzipped his pants. His huge, black cock plopped out and stood straight out. He was hard as wood, and his dick was ebony black in color. It was hot as fuck. He told me to go down on the nasty cock, so I got to my knees and started sucking his horny head. I ran my tongue around the rim making him jerk with pleasure. He moaned in ecstasy. He pushed my head harder and deeper until I was gagging on his big dong.

He then pushed the papers off of his desk and said, “I am going to fuck your brains out Bridgette.” And this he did for sure! He guided me on top, and I screwed him first. I ground on his boner deep and slow making my insides explode in my first pussy squirt. I rose up and came all over him. Then I pounded him hard and fast and gushed again on his horny lap.

He then picked me up, led me against the wall, and proceeded to pound me so fucking hard I was gasping. It felt hot as hell. This was the hottest fuck I had ever had. I could feel by the stiffening of his steel dick that he was going to shoot off inside me. He asked me did I care if he unloaded his horny dick inside and I said no. When I felt his head harden and pop out the first cum wad, I started creaming my cunt, too. Right there not five minutes before class started, Mr. Williams and I had nasty, hot sex and came all over the place. I was still recovering when we heard the first knock on the door. He quickly put his black snake up in his pants, and I lifted my skirt and tried to recover and get a hold of myself. He was still harder than fuck.

I am sure the classroom reeked of hot sex and cum. I saw some on the floor and bent over to wipe it up with a napkin. I flashed every dick and pussy in the room my cum-filled snatch. I heard several moans and saw several hands disappear under their desks. Being a nympho, I had my first spontaneous squirt right there in front of the class, and it trickled onto the floor. I am sure several people came on themselves just watching.

I was so damn horny and dirty that day I couldn't stay in class. It was too sexual and I thought I might attack the dicks and pussies. I walked out knowing girls and guys were jerking and fingering under their desks. I walked back to my dorm with my fingers in my pussy. I didn't care who saw.

When I opened the door to my dorm, I saw my roommate naked and fingering herself off to some pussy porn. When I walked in she started to squirt, and she hit the screen of her computer with her juice. I walked over, licked it up, and then kissed her, and we shared her cunt cum. Her taste made me cum over and over. She and I spent all afternoon being nasty sluts and getting each other off until our pussies had big red swollen lips. I couldn't resist; I went and pulled slowly on my roomies lips with my mouth until she had a squirming body orgasm all over her bed. She then buried her head in my cunt and ate me off one final time. I squirted her down good until her hair was drenched with pussy.

I knew I was going to love college. The fact that I could be the nympho I naturally am just proved it to me. I love sex and I am not ashamed to admit. No pussy or dick is safe as long as I am around and horny. If they are alive, I will fuck them one way or another. Just ask Mr. Williams if you don't believe me.

9 THE EXPERIMENT

I am a starving college student and am always in desperate need of extra cash. I am also very sexually oriented. I am not a nympho, but let's just say I am damn close!

About a year ago, I was really hurting for some extra cash. I had a job but it just wasn't paying enough to pay all of my bills and to let me eat and live comfortably. I noticed on the corkboard in the hallway on campus a poster about signing up to be a "tester" for some new sexual stimulant drugs. It explained that these were new drugs to be tested on men and women to increase libido and help with impotence in males. It was a project the Psychology Department was doing. It was probably something the sex therapy majors were doing for credit. I tore off one of the tabs with the phone number and headed to class.

After my history class, I got my cell phone out and called the number. A male answered the phone. "Hello, this is Dr. Harding. May I help you?"

"Uh-uh yes!" I replied.

I told him what I was inquiring about, and he truly seemed relieved to have a female candidate interested. I could hear it in his voice. He then told me I could meet him in his office in about an hour to discuss the experiment. He also told me that if I made it all the way through, they'd pay me 500 bucks for my trouble.

In exactly an hour, I headed for the Psychology Department building. I finally found Dr. Harding's office. He had a nameplate on his door. I knocked lightly and he opened the door. He was hot as fuck! I expected a nerdy old man wearing horn-rimmed glasses. Boy was I surprised!

He opened the door, introduced himself, and shook my hand. He explained to me that there were three different drugs that were being tested and that the computer would pick one randomly for me. He also explained that I would have to report in every day and let the staff know of any changes or side effects I was having.

Dr. Harding also made sure that I

understood that these test drugs had not yet been approved by the FDA. The medical community was hopeful that these drugs would increase libido in men and women and help with male impotence. I agreed to take part in the experiment and Dr. Harding prepared the paperwork for me to sign. He told me to get some rest and show up the next morning at 9 a.m. on the dot.

I did what he said. I got up the next morning, showered, and prepared for my day. I was kind of excited by this whole thing. I had always been a very sexual being. This was going to be quite a thrill getting to test out new sex enhancement pills. I went in my car and headed for the university campus.

I went to the Psychology Department building and headed for Dr. Harding's office. He opened the door and welcomed me in. His nurse took me to an examination room down the hall and took all of my vital signs. Then she went to get the meds. She brought back a pale pink oval pill and a small Dixie cup of water and instructed me to take it. Then she told me to have breakfast if I hadn't already. I had already eaten two lemon meringue doughnuts from Dunkin' Donuts. After I took the pill, the nurse proceeded to blab about other things I should expect and what to report. Blah, blah, blah. I saw Dr. Harding coming down the hall and he came into where the nurse and I were. He also went over some guidelines, and I must admit I almost fell asleep. I mean, really, how can sex be a negative side effect?

After listening to their spiel, I took my paperwork and info and bebopped out of there. I couldn't help but wonder what might happen to me. What if I got a raging desire to fuck? Would I attack poor unsuspecting freshmen in the hall? Would I jump under desks, give head, and eat out cunts? I thought it would be hilarious if I did. I could just see myself tearing down the halls of the college ripping my shirt off and fingering my hole! Kind of like the Incredible Hulk!

The rest of the day was pretty uneventful until about 1 or 2 in the afternoon. This is when I swear my pussy started to nearly gush wetness. I had always been prone to being naturally lubricated, but this was insane! I don't think it had ever been this wet! I was actually afraid I might just leak out onto the floor. That would have been so embarrassing. I decided I better visit the ladies' room and check this out. I went into a stall and couldn't believe my eyes! I was so wet my panties and pants were soaked through. I was trying to wipe some of the wetness away with tissue when I found myself getting incredibly turned on. There was no way I was leaving that stall without cumming!

I heard other girls coming and going, but how would they know I was fingering my cunt in there? They wouldn't! So I started doing just that. I got a huge thrill out of the idea of maybe someone overhearing. I wasn't used to this type of deviant behavior, but it was sexually delicious. I went after my drenched snatch full force. I rubbed my clit as hard as I possibly could with my soaked index finger. It felt so fucking good I wanted to scream. I don't mean I wanted to moan. I mean I wanted to scream loudly! But I knew I couldn't. I accidentally said "fuck" under my breath. The gal in the stall beside me got real quiet. I wondered if she could smell my cream. The thought of it was enough to send me straight to orgasm land.

I came hard and good and I could only hope that the girls in the adjoining stalls didn't hear me. Then again, I sort of hoped that they did. The thought had an appeal to me that was new. I figured it was because of the test drug. I do believe I was going to enjoy this experiment. How could getting an increased sexual drive be a bad thing?

I drove home that afternoon feeling a bit flushed and my temperature seemed to be higher than usual. At first, I was a bit alarmed and then it hit me. An extreme horny feeling washed over me like nothing ever has before. It made me feel warm from the tips of my toes to the top of my head. The extreme heat coursing through my blood was almost more than I could bear. I could tell that I was going to have to be fucked hard and very soon! My cock hotel was seething with desire. I was dying to have a big, hard, one-eyed trouser snake inside me, and I was bound and determined to get myself one.

I quickly rushed inside my apartment, showered, and changed into a tight little red dress that fit my body snugly and sexily. My passion hole was burning the whole time and ready to get screwed. I hit the nightlife with a mission. My mission was plain and simple: I needed a cunt teaser and I needed one ASAP. I knew it was more than likely because of the test drug, but at that moment, I didn't care. I walked inside my favorite club, "Cabana's," and ordered margarita on the rocks with lots of salt. I noticed a hot black dude sitting at the bar. I had always heard that black men were well hung and had huge peckers. I was about to find out. I had never had the courage to do this before, but I had never taken this medicine before either!

I walked up to him, and believe it or not, I actually rubbed my ultrasensitive nipples up against his shoulders. He turned and looked a bit surprised, but he smiled nonetheless. I couldn't believe the words that came out of my mouth, but before I could stop myself, I said to him, "You want to get fucked? Can I overdose on your hot chocolate?" Before I knew it, this whole evening became a whirlwind and a joy ride. He and I quickly found ourselves in a motel room ripping each other's clothes off.

Let me just say that those rumors I heard proved themselves to be true. When I unzipped the black dude's jeans, the biggest and juiciest snake I had ever had the pleasure of feasting my eyes upon popped out. Before he could utter a word, I was on my knees swallowing his black dick whole. He grabbed my hair, balled it in his fist, and said, "Yeah, baby, suck my black stick." I sucked that dude's cunt fucker so hard he fell back on the bed from the sheer power of my sucking abilities. He grabbed my head and grinded me harder and harder into his dick.

Then before he could say anything, I

was butt naked on top of him riding his hot chocolate box pleaser fast and furious. He was deep inside of me as I squirmed and wiggled on top of his raging meat. This was the best fuck I had ever had. My pussy felt like it might actually catch fire and shoot flames.

It was one of the wildest nights I can remember, and the next morning when I woke up, it kind of felt like a dream. I got ready for class that day, but I first had to stop in to see Dr. Harding and have my vitals checked. I wasn't quite sure what I would tell them. I just knew I had better tell them something. The nurse took me to the examining room and took my vitals, and then Dr. Harding came in and asked me a few questions.

He asked me if I had any sexual side effects, and I explained to him that I did have an increased sex drive, but I certainly didn't go into any detail. I was afraid that if I did, they wouldn't give me another dose. They seemed pleased with my answers, so I was given my next dose. I went about most of my school day again, and it was very uneventful until about the time when I was getting ready to leave. I cannot describe exactly what came over me, but I had strong urges for the same sex. In other words, I was having lesbian thoughts and desires. I had never done this before so I knew it had to be the effects of the drug.

I barely made it inside my apartment without having to relieve my sexual desires. I rushed inside and grabbed my favorite rabbit toy from my dresser drawer. I sat down on the floor in front of the mirror and went after my wet and fervent snatch vigorously. I was absolutely on fire. I thought my cunt might combust right there on the spot. It was a huge turn-on watching my pussy lips swell to a bright flaming red in my mirror. I felt something inside myself I had never felt before. I could tell I was fixing to cum and it was going to be different than I had ever come before. Before I had very much time to think about it, my pussy started to squirt fucking everywhere. I had never gushed or squirted before, but I had heard about it. I had no idea what a sexually erotic treat I was missing out on. My cunt gushed so enormously that my cum hit the mirror in front of me. Just seeing it do that made me hotter than I already was. In fact, it was such a huge turn-on I felt another squirt coming on. There was no way I could stop my box from squirting like crazy again. This time it was so powerful that I writhed in the floor, barely able to contain my orgasm. It felt so good and was so powerful I screamed an erotic cry of sweet release.

Every muscle in my body seemed to be

involved in this orgasm. I felt it surge seemingly endlessly throughout my entire core. This had to be the best orgasm I had ever had, bar none. I still wasn't satisfied though. My cunt was still burning with intense desire like I had never experienced before. I decided to hit the city and go out to a lesbian club. For some reason I had an intense appetite for a female. I wanted to eat pussy and I wanted to eat it now! I went to a lesbian club I had heard several good things about from some girls at school. I was dressed to kill and ready to have the thrill of my life.

I made my way inside, ordered a Tequila Sunrise, and sat down at a small corner table. I noticed a hot blonde eyeballing me from across the room. I could barely keep from sticking my fingers inside my pussy; she was getting me so wet and excited. I watched her making her way across the room. I couldn't believe my eyes, but I thought she was coming towards me. Yes! She was. She walked over and introduced herself, and before I could think straight, I gave her a French kiss and grabbed her tight ass. She asked me if I wanted to go to her place and, of course, I said yes.

We got to her house and barely made it through the door before she had my skirt up and was eating the fuck out of my pussy. No one had ever gone down on me like that before. It felt amazing. I was in ecstasy. She swirled her tongue rapidly around my clit, making it stand up like a small cock. It got hard as hell and I squirted suddenly all over her face and down her throat. I could see she was furiously fingering her own box while she performed oral sex on me. I don't know what was in those pills, but damn it, they made me a flaming nympho!

I led her to the bed and then buried my head into her wet snatch. I drove my tongue deep inside her slit like I had done this a million times. She started to moan and scream, writhing her body all over the bed. I could tell she was enjoying the way I ate the fuck out of her horny puss. It tasted so good and sweet, and when she started to cream, it made me cum again, too. We both started to scream in orgasmic pleasure while both of our red-hot pussies juiced at the exact same time.

The next morning I woke up in my bed, feeling groggy with the smell of tequila and cunt. I started to remember my activities from the night before. I reached down and could feel the cream oozing from my horny hole. I couldn't help but masturbate again and bring myself to another mind-blowing climax. I was really starting to like this sex pill, yes I was. I couldn't wait to get to class and take my third dose. I just wondered what I might do this time. By the way, my wet cunt felt there was no telling.

10 THE BACKBOOTH

My husband and I have been married for almost a year now, but the passion between us is as strong as ever. We have always had an amazing sex life, and a year of marriage hadn't changed that at all. We are going as strong as ever with our kinky, sexual role-play and fun.

One of our favorite things to do is something my husband and I have done since about two weeks after we first started dating. We have a favorite restaurant that we frequent; we even have our very own special back booth. In this booth, we had done all kinds of sexy and kinky things. If you can imagine a sexual act, we have probably done it. We love to explore our deviant side when we go to our booth every week.

One night, I was due to meet my hubby at our restaurant in about half an hour. I was so excited I couldn't wait. It is very thrilling to know that your husband can still turn you on as much as mine does me. I was decked out in my sexiest outfit for our rendezvous. I put on my pink lace corset and my tight black leather miniskirt (with no panties, of course). I also put on my six-inch pink stilettos that gave me that 'come fuck me now' look.

I was looking super hot, if I do say so myself. I got in my minivan and drove to the place my hubby and I loved so much. I was so excited I could feel my cunt getting drenched just thinking about it. I got out of my van and went inside. I had seen my husband's car outside, so I knew he was there waiting for me. I was so happy I could hardly contain my excitement.

I checked in up front and headed back to our booth. There was my husband with a horny grin plastered on his face. I could tell he was hot and ready to fool around. I walked up to him and planted a deep, wet French kiss upon his lips. I lifted my leg, put it on his waist, and made sure to rub my bald cunt on his hips. He replied with an even wetter French kiss and a moan.

We sat down and gave the waitress our drink and food orders. Once the waitress left the table, my husband slowly slid his hand under the table. He snuck his hand underneath my skirt and started to finger my more-than-drenched pussy. I replied with a sultry moan and started moving up and down on his wet fingers. He started with one finger and then slowly added another finger, then another. I was getting increasingly wet and it felt amazing.

He kept fingering me even when the waitress brought our drinks and salads. I love it when we challenge ourselves not to moan when the wait staff comes to our table. It is always fun to see the look on their faces. You can always tell when they are wondering if maybe something naughty is going on. It is funny and a turn-on at the same time. It is a huge part of the thrill wondering just how much other people understand what is going on.

The thought of actually fucking and fondling in public places has always been exciting to me. It was really thrilling since I'd met my hot and horny hubby. He and I had pushed the limit several times right there in that booth, and I had a feeling we would keep pushing our luck to see if we got caught. For me, that is half of the thrill. I think a lot of people fantasize about doing sexual things in public, but most of them are too afraid that they'll be caught. For me, it just makes it all the more tempting and exciting.

Next, I decided to move my hand down my hubby's pants. First, I unzipped his jeans. His dick was so rock-hard it popped right out of his jeans. I could feel the swollen girth with my fingers, and I could practically smell his precum cock cream seeping from the tip. I was dying to dive under the booth and lap away at his prick. I might have done it, too, if I'd had a chance. I looked up to see our curious waitress coming with our steaks. I really went to town jerking my man's meat, then!

He kind of smiled sheepishly at the waitress, holding back a groan. I knew he was dying to let out a huge, bear-like growl. It was all he could do not to pop off in my palm right then and there as the waitress leaned over, revealing her ample cleavage. I wondered if she knew he and I were getting hot and bothered. I also wondered if her cunt was getting wet thinking about it. The thought of it made my cunt almost groan with pleasure. I could swear I smelled my pussy cream as I opened my legs a bit under the top of the table. I kept on jacking my man's wood until I knew it was just about "there," and then I stopped. I knew it would put hubby in the throes of sheer, unadulterated agony. I happen to love doing that, I must admit.

My husband and I ate a bit of our meal; the whole time I made sure to squirm about uncomfortably. When I did that, it rubbed my pussy lips all over the booth cushion. I knew my husband would get wood watching that, and that made my cunt even hornier. I was definitely wishing I had something long, thick, and hard to put inside my candy.

We ate about half of our meal before my husband reached inside a plastic sack he had on the other side of him. I had been wondering what kind of goodies he had in that bag.

He revealed a glossy green cucumber fresh from the market down the street. I was damn near ecstatic. There was nothing like fucking a piece of produce in public with people all around. It was almost like receiving a jolt of adrenaline right on the spot. I slowly slid the cucumber underneath my writhing hips. I could barely contain myself—I was so horny. I slowly inched the green dick inside of me, letting out a soulful whimper. My hubby put his index finger to his lips, reminding me to be quiet. I looked over at an older couple at a table across from us. I could swear the older man had a horny look on his face.

Whether he truly did or not remained a mystery, but just the thought of it urged me on to keep screwing the smooth green cock. I was getting lost in the fuck I was receiving and failed to notice the waitress at my right side. My hubby nudged me with his elbow, as if to say, "Cut it out!" When I noticed her, I suddenly stopped fucking it. I kind of grinned and took a big long sip of my Tequila Sunrise.

I was poised on the brink of an amazing orgasm. I literally had to squeeze my legs together to hold back from having one. I am sure that I was visibly trembling and that the waitress definitely noticed. The cuke stuck out like some lewd alien cock from the clutches of my twitching pussy, one end clenched tightly between my creamy thighs. One wrong move and it would be coated with creamy, raunchy ranch dressing.

When the nosy waitress finally walked away from our table, I removed the cucumber painstakingly slowly and put it to my mouth real quick to lick my cream off. My hubby almost had a nut right then. I love messing with people's heads in public, especially when it involves my furry snatch and produce.

I could tell my husband was doing something lewd under the table, so when it seemed like no one in the restaurant was paying attention, I took a quick glance to see for myself. He was playing with the head of his luscious dick. I could see him doing circles around the rim with his forefinger. It was such a turn-on for me to see my husband do this. It was fucking hot as hell actually.

I looked at my hubby and he had "that look" in his eyes—the look that told me I was going to get the banging of my life when we got home. As he played with his dick head, I was tempted to stick my fingers back inside my now-soaked cunt. As I plunged my fingers in, I was tempted to fist myself. But then I had a better idea. I leaned over and whispered my plan into my man's ear.

He reached innocuously up under my skirt and found my furry pussy soaked with wetness. As he slipped a finger between my lips, I again whispered in his ear.

"I need to cum sooo bad."

He glanced around nervously before taking my hand in his and leading me to the restrooms. Glancing around to make sure no one saw, he pushed me hurriedly into the men's room and into a stall. I nearly fell into the toilet. Immediately, he had my dress over my head. My spread cunt was oozing with need, and my lips were swollen to a glowing red.

He slowly but assuredly began to plunge his throbbing member deep into my waiting slit. The first entrance of his raging dick is always the best. I reached back to cup his cum-filled balls and twisted them slightly as he plunged deeper and deeper into my screaming cunt. I begged him to push himself as deep as possible into my gushing chasm.

He was jabbing his horny cock into my hole, blending erotic pleasure with sexually satisfying pain. My pussy lips were throbbing, bold red against the whiteness of the bathroom. I simply could not get enough of this man.

His hands were on my writhing hips. With each thrust, the sound of wet flesh smacking wet flesh echoed through the empty bathroom. He reached around me and pulled by dress away from my burning tits, his fingers pulling and twisting my aching nipples. I could feel my cunt tightening around his cock. My pussy was a raging, throbbing mass of fiery heat.

His dick felt like a glowing hot stick of fire. It made my pussy steam as it was thrust in and out of me from behind. As he pounded and banged me faster and harder, I could feel my cream beginning to build inside my hot, writhing body. I knew when my pussy did gush, it was going to be a mass explosion of dripping cream. My hubby's breathing had taken on a raspy and animalistic sound, hot against the bare skin of my back.

His chin was scratching against my upper ass, causing a sensation that was curiously and amazingly sexual in nature. He continued to thrust his bulging member deep into my cunt hole. He was fucking my brains out by this time. And I loved every fucking hot minute of it, too. There is nothing quite as thrilling as getting screwed in a public restroom, knowing every minute that you might get caught.

I could feel his nads getting harder and stiffer as he boinked the living daylights out of me. It was going to be an explosive orgasm for both of us when it happened. He was pounding his raging meat in me so hard my tits were bouncing furiously against each other. They were actually starting to throb; they were hitting each other so hard.

I was reaching and grabbing for anything I could possibly find to hold onto while I got the banging of my life! The toilet back was my best option, and it was about to fall off as he was screwing me so voraciously. I didn't want that to happen, so I flipped my body around, bending his cock inside me. I stood up and he lifted me by my hips and pinned me against the wall of the stall. I wrapped my milky thighs around his waist and allowed him the deepest entrance of his dick yet.

This was the best fuck my hubby and I

had ever enjoyed.

Then suddenly, we hear the bathroom door open. He quickly pulls out and holds his balls tight. I jump up on top of the toilet, standing there in my pink stilettos. I am squeezing my raging cunt shut as tight as possible. We were both on the nerve-wracking verge of squirting.

With a devious grin, he buried his head in my cum-soaked hairy cunt. I literally had to hold my mouth shut to keep myself from screaming in nasty, erotic ecstasy. He was eating me out like a pro, and I was about to scream as it felt so damn hot. My lips were on the verge of a creamy, cum-induced surrender.

He buried his face in my snatch and turned it side to side so vehemently I could hardly see his fucking head. Suddenly I knew my cunt was going to blow. I couldn't contain my spit a moment longer. I was foaming at the lips. That's when I let the dam loose and let it flow. I creamed all over my husband's moustache, drenching his chin and face. He was lapping it up as quickly as I was dishing it out. He let out a quiet moan.

Then, the other dude left the stall and my hubby plunged his raging meat deep inside me. With two quick thrusts, he came inside me. He grabbed my hair and pulled hard as he closed his eyes and groaned out a satisfied bellow.

We then embraced and gave each other a warm, lingering French kiss. My hubby whispered in my ear, “I love you, baby. You are so fucking hot.” He pinched my tushy as we snuck out of the bathroom hand in hand and headed to our car in the parking lot.

As we drove away, I thought, “He is so getting laid when we get home!”

11 PARTY FAVORS

I am a slave to lust and a virtual slave to cock. I will admit I adore cock, and the more I get of it, the more I want it. That is why Jack is the best boyfriend I could possibly have. Jack is a man-whore and has tons of male friends. I am a slave to Jack and his sexual needs. If he wants me to fuck and suck his friends, I do it no questions asked.

This particular night, we had a big party planned, and I was going to be the only favor given. I was glad to do it, I might add. I was dressed to kill for the occasion, looking hot as hell. I had on my leather collar, a tight and short black leather mini-skirt, and knee-high come fuck me boots. I had my long red hair curled and teased. Jack didn't make me do his friends. I wanted to do it. I am a slut and proud to be one. I was looking too hot to handle even if I do say so myself.

Before Jack's friends started to arrive, Jack questioned me and looked me over closely. He lifted up my mini-skirt to reveal my bare, shaved snatch. He smiled seemingly pleased that I wasn't wearing any panties. He also gave my pussy a few finger fucks before dropping my skirt back just about one quarter inch under my tight ass. Then he un-snapped my leather, sleeveless vest. Of course, my perky tits popped right out. I didn't own a bra. I never wore one.

Jack asked me what I planned to do this evening at the party. I told him I was going fuck and suck as much cock as I possibly could. He smiled, nodded his head, and said, "That's my girl." I smiled back seductively, turned around, flashed my tight booty in his face, and wiggled it sexily.

Jack then told me that he had an extra request on this particular night. I said, "Sure anything for you, Boo." He told me that I had to swallow every single drop of cum I could possibly get my mouth on this night. No spitting or letting any spray on my body. I was to swallow it all. I of course agreed and told him I had zero problems doing that.

I went into the bathroom and did a few

extra touch ups on my appearance. I even decided to add a pair of thigh-high fishnets stocking to my look and a pair of fishnet gloves as well. I looked like a slut extraordinaire. I looked good enough to eat and fuck. Suddenly, I heard the doorbell. Yippee I thought, our first cock is here!

"Come get the door baby!" I heard Jack yell. I traipsed my hot ass up to the door and flung it open. There stood Jack's friend Sean. Sean was a big black dude with a cock about 8 and a half inches long, and he was built like a brick house.

Sean's arrival made my pussy drip instantly. He was my favorite cock to partake of. I secretly wished his cock was all mine. He was hung, horny, and hot as hell. I went up to Sean and gave him a sexy, wet kiss with loads of tongue. He loved it. I could tell by the growth I felt in his Armani jeans that he was happy to see me and horny as fuck. I reached my hand down to his cock and gave it a grope through his pants. Sean said 'mmmmm' and stuck his thumb under my skirt, pushed on my clit a few times. I felt wetness flood my pussy. It doesn't take a rocket scientist to figure out that Sean and I were going to have a fuck-filled night together. Sean and I had gotten into each other so much that we failed to close the door, and I looked up to see his homey Jerome standing there with a big grin plastered across his face. I could tell by the look on his face he was in need of some of what Sean had just gotten.

I walked over to Jerome, grabbed his hand, and led him into the house. I shut the door behind him. I laid a big wet kiss on Jerome too. By the feel of his crotch pressed against mine, I could tell he was getting turned on too. It was hard to choose which one of these guys I liked best and which cock. Sean was hugely endowed that's for sure, and Jerome was too. It was a very close call between the two. I might just have them lay their cocks side by side once, so I could measure them. How kinky would that be? I was such a bad girl and I loved it.

I pulled Jerome's ear close to my mouth and whispered, "Would you like to get fucked tonight?" His eyes got huge along with his cock as he said, "Of course I would, baby." That's when Sean piped in and said, "Hey man she fucks me first." I kind of snickered, but I could tell Sean was fucking serious as a heart attack. That's when Jack walked over and said, "Hey dudes, she's my woman and I say who she fucks first." I laughed. It felt hot being the center of attention.

I was about to make a cute little comment when I heard the bell. I said, "I guess another prick has arrived." I shook my ass to the door and could practically "hear" the cocks get hard as I passed by the three of them with their tongues wagging. I swung the door open to reveal one of Jack's football buddies, Evan. I gave Evan a huge smile, dropped to my knees, and licked the outside of his jeans right where I could see his dick was lying. He let out a moan and pulled me up by my hair, planted a French kiss on my lips. I will say Evan was a real hottie, one of the best at eating pussy.

I now had four cocks here and that was a great place to start the party. I was ready to get this party going. I led the guys into the living room and took their drink requests. Once everyone had a stiff drink, I decided to work on getting even stiffer cocks in the room. I stood up and decided to do a little dance I learned from my former days of being a stripper.

I laid on the sex appeal, and I could tell the cocks were standing up to attention. Next, I instructed them to take their pants off. Then I told them to start stroking their members slowly and methodically. I watched on and then lifted my tiny skirt to reveal a near-hissing cunt underneath. I stuck my index and middle finger inside my hole and did some fancy finger work.

Fuck! It felt good! I pulled my two fingers out to reveal two cream-drenched digits to the watching cocks. As sexily as possible, I licked my cream off my fingers as slowly as I could. I swear, the cocks visibly increased at least an inch apiece. I then decided to walk over to the 4 eager cocks staring at me like kids in a licorice shop. I looked at Jack who nodded a yes with his head. I first when over to Jack and did a little hand job before I buried his dick in my throat all the way to his gonads. He groaned a pleasurable sound and then tapped my head. When he tapped my head, it meant he wanted me to go down the line doing something similar. I next moved onto my favorite homeboy, Sean. I loved the taste of his chocolate meat. The head on it was amazing, and I swear his dick was as wide as a pop can across it. Once I got started on Sean's dick, it was hard to let up. This black dude just had the most delicious cock in the world.

Sean threw his head back against the couch cushion thoroughly enjoying what I was doing to his swollen prick. He put his head on my red hair and guided me the way he wanted his throbbing member to be sucked and licked. He lifted up his brown hips, which thrust his gargantuan dick even further down my throat. I wished I could finish this dark joystick off right this second, but I knew Jack would want me to move on down the line.

So, next comes Sean's homeboy Jerome. I loved his big black dick too. It was amazingly long, but still didn't have the massive girth of Sean's. It tasted like mocha though, and he came wads and wads of thick creamy cum when he came. I licked the fuck out of his shaft up and down and had him wanting to nut. Then I figured before he let go of a big juicy load in my mouth I better move onto the jock Evan.

Evan had wide eyes, and I could tell he was eagerly waiting for me to get my bright red lips on his dick. I smiled seductively at Evan and teased my way down his shaft barely grazing it. I then grazed my tongue back up and tickled the edges of his rim with my tongue. Evan actually jerked and squirmed like a chic getting her clit licked. Just about the time I thought he'd nut all over the place, I quit and stood up.

Jack motioned his head towards the table beside the couch. I knew this meant I was supposed to get my rabbit vibrator and turn these dudes on even more. If that was even possible! I walked over to the table drawer and got my hot pink rabbit out. I laid down on the coffee table and hiked up my mini skirt up. I could see the four cocks watching me adamantly, excited about the little sideshow I was about to put on for them. I was doing my best to turn them on more!

I started working my cat pretty furiously, while these horny-as-fuck dudes watched on, speechless. I really knew how to work my pussy with a toy. I had tons of experience with it, and I had been masturbating since I was a teen girl. I moaned and writhed all over the table for the express purpose of turning these dicks on so much they would beg for more.

I also hoped it would make them beg to pound the fuck out of my pussy. I must admit I wanted to get banged by every dick in the house. I was a horny slut with carnal needs that were nearly impossible to quench. It took more than one big prick to please my womanly sexual desires. Hell, I wasn't even sure that these four cocks could please me. I was lost in thought about cocks and plunging the vibe in my snatch, when I heard Jack clear his throat. Sometimes, I liked to tease Jack and refer to him as my master. So I promptly answered, "Yes, Master?"

"Why don't you head for the bedroom baby and we'll bring our cocks right behind you."

"Sure, Master, anything you want." I replied. I was anxious to take these dicks on like a woman. I had huge plans for these boners. If they only knew how huge my plans were!

The five of us all headed for Master Jack's huge bedroom. I may have forgotten to mention that Jack is a very rich man and lives lavishly. So when you visit his house, you can count on having an exquisite and outlandish time. His bedroom was in the style of a classic yet exotic bachelor pad. He had mirrors on the ceiling, and he even had the pink champagne on ice just like the song says! In fact, he popped the cork, and we all passed the bottle taking big swigs of the bubbly libation.

Jack motioned to the bed, so I walked over to it and removed my clothing, piece by piece, as the dicks drooled. I then told them to think of a number between 1 and 10 and whoever came closest to my number came to greet me on the bed first. Should they tie, those two would then think of a number and so on. I thought of a number, and they wrote theirs down on paper and, what do you know, my big black dream man won. I got the pleasure of fucking and sucking Sean first. Then Evan came second, and I would probably get them both at the same time as well.

Sean walked over to the bed and immediately jumped my bones. That's what was so hot about this guy. He had confidence that his cock was good enough to please me and so much more. He had all the right moves. He kissed very wet and passionately, and he slowly eased his big fucking dick in me. He felt so damn good I almost came when he entered. He fucked me every which way but loose. About the time he was banging my pussy good, I saw Jack motion Evan over to take my ass. I was sandwiched between a black dick and a white prick, and it felt so damn good. I could feel my pussy wanting to cum, but I wasn't about to let it yet.

I was getting pounded in both directions hard and furious. My tits were jiggling, but Sean managed to suck them anyway. He pulled my nips with his mouth with just a bit of teeth and it felt amazing. He plunged his nasty black dong harder and faster, while Evan copied the tempo with his fat white peter. I looked up and could tell the other two cocks were seething in their cock juice and their dick heads were drooling.

Jack snapped his fingers, and Evan and Sean started jerking their cocks on each side of the bed, while Jack and Jerome started anticipating their moves. I didn't have time to think before Jerome had plunged his huge black dick down my hungry throat. I made him switch places with me, so I could bend over his cock with my ass up in the air for Master Jack to bang. As I sucked the hell out of this black dude's dong, I got torn a new one by Jack. He fucked me so hard I winced but I loved it. I could feel Jack's balls draw up against my tight little ass. I knew this meant he was going to shoot his first load of semen.

Jack starting grinding more ferociously, and Jerome made another ram into my mouth with his bulging black meat. I couldn't even make a gulping sound because this dick was so big. I reached down and middle fingered my clit as fast as I could. I saw the other two guys about to pull their dicks off. They were so damn horny. I looked up at them with desire and lust in my eyes. I felt like a female animal getting gang banged like this. This was so erotic I started to cum for the first big time that evening. The more I came, the faster I fingered my clit. I flicked feverishly and made it squirt big time. I really thought I might soak the ceiling in cunt juice.

The thought of that was so damn hot that right when I felt another orgasm coming I jumped away from the dick, stood up, and squirted my slit all over the side of the bed and the rug under my feet. It felt amazing to do this. The more I squirted, the more I wanted to have this hot cunt fucked. The cocks looked on with bright eyes and a couple of them spontaneously popped off in their hands. Those two happened to be Sean and Jerome, respectively.

I knew there were plenty of more exciting sexual activities in store for us 5, and I looked to my master to choose the next lustful act we would partake of. Then Jack blurted out, "Well boys and girl, I do believe I am going to crank up my movie camera for the next sexual encounter."

I looked at Jack with a face that I knew would clue him in on exactly what I was in the mood for. Since I had just had cocks coming in both of my holes, I was in the mood to get eaten out. I don't mean just my pussy eaten either. I loved my anus licked and fucked with a tongue as well. The idea of a nasty cock eating another cock's cream out of my holes excited me immensely. So my three well hung boy toys and I headed over to Jack's king-sized bed for some fucking good fun.

I laid my sexy, nude ass back on some fluffy throw pillows and spread my legs just as wide as I could possibly make them. I toyed with my clit for a few just to make the cocks salivate even more. Who wants to eat me out first as I revealed some thick white pussy cream from the inner folds of my labia. The dicks all at once looked like they were waiting in line at the ice cream stand.

I must admit, I hoped that Sean made it over to my gaping slit first. He was all that and so much more. He was a tiger in bed but also very sexy and gentle. Look and behold, it did look like Sean was the most eager to attack my beaver. He first took his nimble tongue and drew figure eights around my clit that had just peaked out from her pink rosy hood.

It felt so good having his hot mouth all over my peach sucking my juices up. It had been a long time since I had my pussy eaten out very good. Sean knew exactly how to eat my snatch to make me writhe around uncontrollably. While Sean had his face buried in my love box, Jerome walked over and thrust his big meat right down my throat. It was an amazing feeling being the meat in this lust sandwich.

Sean's intensity between my legs grew, and so did Jerome's, straight down my hungry throat. I could taste the first few drops of Jerome's precum, and I knew he was about to have an orgasm. It just made me hornier as it intensified the pelvic contractions deep inside my body. I knew I was about to squirt again, all of it in Sean's mouth. I arched my hips upward and thrust my pussy into Sean's face, hard. He groaned a sound of sexual pleasure, and I could see he was jacking on his cock while lapping up my cream.

We all then started to climax at once, and it was incredibly erotic. I was pushing my cunt into Sean, Sean was jerking his cock furiously, and Jerome was groaning in loud orgasmic pleasure as the three of us all came at once. In the throes of my amazing orgasm, I looked over to see Evan and Jack playing with their dicks, each eagerly awaiting a turn to devour my body and my pussy.

I looked at Jack and could see he was dying to take me and screw me hard. I motioned with my finger for him to 'come here', and he walked over and without saying a word plunged his rock solid cock up my ass. I stood there with my hands against the wall. I pushed my tight ass out and backed into his dick even more, making it swell to mass proportions. Then Evan walked over to my left side as I. He wanted me to suck him hard. I was all too happy to oblige.

Jack led me to the bed where he thrust his hard as hell cock inside my pussy. Evan got on his knees and wagged his cock over my head. I quickly reached up for it and he bent down and plunged it into my throat. You could tell he desperately wanted his cock sucked big time. His dick was hungry for a wet mouth to get it the fuck off. I looked over at Sean and could see he wanted a piece of the action. I whispered into Jack's ear that I wanted to be fucked by him and Sean at the samc time. He understood and guided me over on my side, and he verbally invited Sean into our action.

Once again, I found myself being serviced in both holes by two delicious cocks at the same time. I had Sean getting his dick sucked along with his buddy Jerome. I cannot say what a hot turn on it was to be the center of attention with 4 dicks at once. I felt like a complete slut, and I absolutely loved it. There is nothing quite like the sensation of all holes being filled all at once.

I looked into my Master's eyes and noticed he had "that look" and I knew exactly what it meant. It meant he wanted to get out the real heavy artillery. I managed to unlock myself from the 4-man sandwich I was in and went to the closet. I got out the handcuffs and the ankle cuffs. I handed them to Jack. He was more than happy to cuff me spread eagle on the bed.

This was going to be very kinky and exciting. Jack instructed the guys that they would each take turns eating me out and getting me right to the point I'd squirt and then back off. He also said that he would go last and maybe he would let me cum if I was a good girl. Jack looked over at Jerome and told him he could eat me first.

Jerome walked over to the bed and went down on me, head first into my horny pussy. It felt so good I almost came on the spot. This guy did magic tricks with his tongue and it felt amazing. He first did little circles and flicks with his tongue and my clit jumped and tingled. He then reached down and spread my lips with his tongue, the tip pulling my swollen clit into his mouth. As he sucked my stiff bud, I screamed, my pussy planted tightly against his mouth, my eyes begging him to bury his thick fingers deep inside me. I could feel my pussy just about to splash everywhere, and I could smell my juices fill the room. Just about that time, Jack motioned for Sean to come over and do his tongue work on me.

As I have said many times, Sean was my favorite of the 4 guys. He had a way of making my clit swell up like a miniature dick on my cunt. It was also easy to see that Sean adored eating pussy. I could feel it by every flick of his hot tongue. He took his time and ate me just how I liked. I wish I could get my hands free and push his head down on me harder. But of course, the cuffs kept me from being able to do that, and it was amazing torture. It was torture that felt hot and horny.

Sean teased my clit like it had never been teased before, and as he did this, he ran his tongue deep inside my hole driving my cunt to places of pure horniness that it had never been before. I could smell and almost taste my pussy as it drew near to an orgasm. In fact, Sean got some of my juices on his fingers and let me have a taste of my own precum. I almost lost all control it tasted so damn good. I needed to squirt so damn bad and it made me writhe around on Jack's bed in torture.

Just about that time, Jack signaled for Evan to come and take over. Evan was busy wanking the fuck out of his dick. Without taking his hand off of his cock, Evan walked over and plunged his head between my legs. Fuck! It felt so good. He pulled on his cock at the same time he sucked my swollen pussy lips. They were standing up to attention big and pink. He took the end of his hot tongue, teased, and tickled the fuck out of each lip separately. I about went wild and crazy at this point. I tried and tried to break free from the cuffs. All three of the other guys looked on with such a lusty look in their eyes. They were seething with pure animal lust; it was easy to see. I soooo badly wanted all of their dicks inside me. It is hard to describe the raw animal lust I myself was feeling. I was hornier than I had ever been before.

I looked over at Jack. I knew he was probably about to bust a nut at this point. I could practically smell his testicles producing dick cum. The room reeked of sex. It was an extremely erotic thing. I guess you just had to be there. All the while, Evan continued to flick away at my lips, making me buck like a bronco. Then he started to do tongue plunges inside my cunt. I looked over and saw all 3 of the other guys jerking wildly at their dicks. Everyone was just about to cum all over the place. Jack looked at Jerome, and Jerome came over to me and squirted all over my face.

I lapped away trying to get every taste of his cum that I could. The more I did that, the more he groaned loudly. It was almost more than I could handle. Then Jack looked over at Sean as if to say, it's your turn dude. So then, Sean walked over to me and unloaded his huge black love stick all over my face and mouth too. A big splash of it hit my mouth, and I ate it up in pure sexual enjoyment. Jack then had that look that I knew so well in his eyes. This meant he wanted his turn at eating my greedy cunt.

He pushed Evan off of me and Jack went down on me. He ate me out like a starving dog that hadn't been fed in a week. He was absolutely ravenous for my pussy cream. Evan walked over above my head and started jerking off all over me. He was so horny. You could see it in his eyes. He stared intently into mine as he unloaded everywhere. I couldn't help it; I let some of my pussy cream go at this time. Jack raised up and said "bad girl" you know better than that. So he quit eating me out. He then told the other 3 guys to get lost. He instructed them to get dressed and head back to where they came from. This is when Jack led me into the bathroom. He had removed my ankle cuffs but left my handcuffs in place. I was so horny and so much in need of an orgasm I was about to lose my mind. He took a paddle and gave me a few swats on my ass for being such a bad girl and squirting off some like I had just done. Jack then turned on the shower and got the water temperature to lukewarm. He led me to the shower and told me to step inside. He then slid the see-through door closed.

As I submerged my head under the shower, I could see Jack really jerking his cock off as hard as he could. I knew I was in store or a huge turn on. My hands were still in cuffs, so there was no way I could touch my hurting pussy. He suddenly started squirting his cock off all over his side of the shower door. I was so turned on by this. I almost spontaneously combusted. I heard Jack say “Lick my cum baby from your side of the door.” He knew I would be teased so much it would make me ache. I started to lick though. I licked and lapped at every spot on my door trying to taste his delicious fluids. Of course, I didn’t get a taste. I could see it sliding down the door, and there was nothing I could do about it but writhe in my misery. I wanted to taste his cum so bad I couldn’t stand it. I also was in desperate need of an orgasm.

Jack opened the door and turned off the water. He then led me to the bedroom with a twinkle in his eyes. I knew what that twinkle meant. He was finally going to let me cum again. He led me to the bed and removed the handcuffs. Jack then went down between my thighs like a rabid animal. He first started pulling on my lips so slowly I almost cried. The suspense of an impending orgasm was delicious torture. I began to thrash my body from side to side. I almost passed out the pleasure was so intense.

I started at that time rubbing my cunt all over his face in voracious up and down motions. I wanted to make sure and mark him with my pussy scent. He actually stuck his nose deep inside my pussy getting a good smell of it. He then pulled back and yanked on my clit hard with his mouth. He even threw in a few nibbles like I liked. Suddenly, I felt him slide his fist inside my cunt and grinding in a painful yet pleasurable motion. In fact, I almost passed out from the combination of pleasure and pain.

He twisted and turned his fist deep inside me, causing a delicious torture like no other I had ever had before. When I exploded, my cunt grabbed his hand so hard with convulsions he cried out in pain, every spasm made my entire body shake like an animal. I looked down to see my cream running all over his wrist. I refused to let go of his balled wrist with my pussy.

'It's better than handcuffs, isn't it Jack?' I

said to him with an evil grin on my flushed face. All Jack could do was nod his head and groan as I laid back on the pillow feeling nothing but ecstasy.

AUTHOR'S NOTE

Readers: I want to expand a few of the stories to see where the characters can be explored further. If there are any of the stories that you would like to read more about again, I'd love to hear from you!

Visit my blog at www.tenaseldan.com

Join my newsletter for free exclusive previews www.tenaseldan.com/in

Follow me on Twitter at www.twitter.com/tenaseldan

Like my page on Facebook at www.facebook.com/tenaseldan

Discover my books at major ebook retailers everywhere.

www.ingramcontent.com/pod-product-compliance
Lightning Source LLC
LaVergne TN
LVHW051004080826
845145LV00009B/2456
* 9 7 8 1 6 2 3 2 7 5 6 9 3 *